PROLOGUE

Located in the middle of the Atlantic Ocean, between Africa and Cuba, and edging north of the Equator is Aronia, one of the most beautiful groups of islands in the world. In the centre of the main island sits a colossal volcano named Oden. Towering fourteen thousand feet above Aronia, Oden looks as though it is part pyramid and appears to be a guardian watching over the small group of islands. A thin cloud of vapour generates from the opening of the volcano, encircling the top, giving the impression of a halo that is symbolic of the angelic island that lies below. Oden evenly descends downward with terrace farming producing thousands of plateaus, like giant fertile green steps the Gods have carpeted to comfort their feet as they ascended the stairs to heaven.

A beautiful lush green forest filled with colourful exotic birds flying high in the tree tops surrounds the base of the volcano. This forest reaches out towards the ocean like a giant green arm with a cupped hand. Flowing down the centre, a silver vein of water cascades over the edge of the green thumb of the cupped hand into a pool of crystal clear water that widens out into a great lake. Trickling streams drain out of this great lake taking the water to its final destination which is the light blue bay on the oceanic beach of Aronia.

In these ancient times, the island looked like a postcard of the most tranquil, serene place on the earth. This was because the island was populated at that time by a society of farmers, fishermen, and hunters. The Aronians' isolated location created an oasis that had never had to suffer the atrocities of war.

A Social Political Fiction novel that's
fun to read

Socrates
Weeps
AS
Plato
Grins

By

Leslie Bruce
Irwin

Table of Contents

Prologue .... pg 3
I The Great Book... pg 5
II King Dominique IV .... pg 13
III The Erikson Family .... pg 32
IV Oh Canada .... pg 44
V A Day in the Life of the King..................... pg 63
VI Chance of a Lifetime............................... pg 62
VII The Proposition...................................... pg 117
VIII The Immigrant ....pg 135
IX Could Things Get Any Worse .... pg 140
X Erikson Expedition .... pg 163
XI The Plan is Coming Together .... pg 193
XII Brian Can't catch a Break.....................,...pg 205
XIII The Erikson Tower 1992 .... pg 214
XIV Brian's Big Day....................................... pg 235
XV The Royals get their Mine .... pg 240
XVI Brian Finds Success but Not Peace....... pg 245
XVII Peder's Seeds of Success .... pg 255
XVIII King Reveals Plan .... pg 260
XIX Erikson's World .... pg 265
XX Stubborn, Bullheaded Old Fool .... pg 268
XXI Election 2040 .... pg 275
XXII The Exodus .... pg 289
About the Author .... pg 296
References and other reading .... pg 298

This is a work a fiction. All of the characters, organizations,

and events portrayed in this novel are products of the authors'

imagination or are used fictitiously.

First Edition

ISBN -978-0-9878848-0-0

Chapter I

THE GREAT BOOK

Domi Olafur I, who was the son of the Aronian tribe's Physician and History Keeper, had first learned to read Futhark and a little of the ancient Latin from the books his father had shown him when he was only four-years-old. He was the first to learn Spanish and was able to speak to the Conquistadors after they had taken the Island. At just ten years of age, Domi was the Conquistadors' translator and the negotiator for the plantation owners and the governor who controlled the mines.

Domi was educated by the Spanish. After teaching himself to fully comprehend Latin, Domi read every book that he could find. The transition from learning medicine from his father, to the languages, the culture, and the sciences of the Spanish, was very easy for him to accomplish. He was fascinated by their tools, weapons, advanced knowledge, and ability to create and shape metals in ways that the Aronians did not know about. Domi learned which rocks could be crushed down and added with sulphur to make gun powder. Since Aronians usually drank wine made from the grapes grown on Vinland Island, he acquired the knowledge of how they made rum from the sugar cane. Domi loved to learn and when he was not translating for the Governor, the Governor had him educated in ways that would best serve the needs of the Spanish and to help to control the Aronians.

The brutality of the Spanish, towards the Aronians, was atrocious. In a society where everyone was equal and all shared in the everyday duties of life, the way in which the Spanish used the Aronians, as disposable tools to accomplish their wants and desires in their quest for gems, sugar, and minerals, was not a concept that the Aronians understood, nor accepted. They fought the Spanish authority constantly. Many Aronians fled to the forest and attacked the Conquistadors when they ventured too far from their fort. The outcome of these battles was usually not good for the Aronians.

Because Domi was serving the Spanish, he had been well looked after; however, Domi's allegiance to his people was never a question in his mind. Moving forward, and learning new and better ways was important to him, but never at the cost of his own people's suffering or death. Domi determined to set out on a plan to free his fellow Aronians and to rid the island of the Spanish.

Through watching the Spanish, Domi learned deception, cunning and brutality. Through his position with the Spanish, he was able to have full access to all the Aronians and to the trouble makers in particular. This enabled Domi to organize all the Aronians in a plot. He quelled all the rebellions on the Island. The Aronians introduced chocolate to the Spanish and served them without question. The Governor rewarded Domi with privileges and favours. Three years passed and the Spanish lived peacefully and comfortably. The Aronians were allowed more privileges and better living standards as long as their productivity stayed up; and, productivity did go up. Most of the mined goods and cultivated crops in Aronia were sent back to Spain. Aronia was spared enough to live, to build buildings and fortifications around the harbour for the Spanish. Canons, swords, muskets, and tools were all produced for the Conquistadors and the Spanish.

On June, twenty-eighth, 1529, the Spanish went to sleep in their safe beds, never to wake up again.

The rebellion was quick, quiet and brutal. Hundreds of Conquistadors, plantation owners, miners, and the Governor were killed. Their throats were slit in their sleep. A small skirmish, with the Conquistadors that tended to the night watch and the ships, broke out. They were so incredibly outnumbered by the Aronians that the battle ended with only a few injuries to Domi's people. The Conquistadors surrendered, but were executed. None were to escape. Domi, at twenty-one years of age, had the entire Aronian nation act as one, with one purpose, and one goal. He had achieved, without casualties, the extermination of every Spaniard in Aronia. This success was one of the contributions to Domi's belief system, his book, and therefore the doctrine of a country.

Domi built a Navy using the Spanish galleons and merchant ships. The ships did not need to be made for long high sea journeys, so he refurbished them to be lighter and more manoeuvrable. He also armed the merchant ships with canons. Domi had the Aronians build hundreds of canons which lined the shores of his island. He had coal and sulphur mined from Vinland Island and had it stored on Aronia Island. He expanded the defenses the Spanish had built and started training the Aronian's in the ways of war. They worked together as a fine oiled machine, each person with a job, with no one man's duty being more important than another man's duty. Domi had managed to get the Spanish to unknowingly equip him with the weapons, the battlements and the ships.

It took some time for the King of Castile and the Spanish to realize that things were amiss. Their merchant ships had left Spain with supplies, and were to pick up their cargo in Aronia, but, none of the ships had returned. The King sent the Conquistadors to investigate and to take back the Island if that was what was necessary. By that time, Domi had built a Navy and an Army that could defend itself against any attack. The defences were impenetrable around the harbour, which was the only way to land on the island. The Spanish tried to set up base camps on the smaller islands, but they were unable to get the camps established or fortified well enough to stop the raids. In the end, the raids supplied Domi with more weaponry, and eventually, gave him a fortress of his own on Vinland Island.

Spain's one advantage was their seemingly unlimited supply of Conquistadors. Domi worried about losing the war to a slow demise of winning battles, even though he lost far less man power than the Spanish lost. After four years, the Spanish threat ended with an accord being signed by Domi and the King of Castile. The Aronians agreed to fully supply Spain with cocoa, sugar, kiwis, bananas, and other exotic fruits for a set price, in gold, that was fair to both the Aronians and the Spanish.

Domi used his education to build the Aronian society by instituting one of the first school systems, in order to educate and teach every Aronian how to read and write. He had the plantations built larger and made them more efficient. He used the materials from the mines to build defences, housing, roads, and bridges. Ships were built, not just for war, but also for trade and exploration. Domi started a trade network of cocoa, sugar, rum, coconuts, bananas, and kiwis. Later, coffee would rival the sugar trade. Domi, now known as King Domi, sat down and wrote "The Great Book" to teach his son and to guide him and the Aronians, to a better way of life. It was the book that would guide the Aronian culture from that day forward.

Domi, had his son, Domi II, travel the world. He sought out trade opportunities and gathered any technological and scientific advancement he could find to add to the Aronian society. Domi II became a student of politics and manipulation. He recognized the value of relationships with other countries; not only to benefit the people of Aronian with minerals and products that they could not get on the island, but to gain security from aggressors, such as the British and the French, who may have wanted the peaceful islands for their own use. He forged alliances with all, and thus, he was able to keep any one nation from overtaking the islands for themselves. As long as other countries were dependent upon the chocolate, sugar, rum, exotic fruits, vegetables, and coffee, the Aronians would be safe. As long as there was more than one country of power, no one country would be allowed to control Aronia.

Aronia's neutrality kept them safe from aggression. It also helped their economy. When war broke out between two other countries, trade with both sides would increase. Gun powder and ships were the largest increase. Aronia had developed their ship building market naturally. In the beginning, ships were built to defend Aronia, then, they were built for trade. Later, the need to build high seas battle ships to protect their merchant ships and shipping lanes from pirates became necessary. The Aronians had earned a reputation as being one of the world's best ship builders. During this time, there was a market for schooners, merchant ships and battle ships that were fast and strong. In the future, this market would change to oil rigs, yachts, cruise ships, frigates, and cargo ships.

This rich history provided the infrastructure the Aronians required to take full advantage of the industrial revolution when it arrived. They were quick to adapt to new ideas and innovations. With a religious idealism of working together as one, to make things better for everyone, they rapidly adjusted to using mechanization, output and throughput. The shipping and trade routes had been established for over two centuries. The quality of their products and the ability to supply all nations had built a world confidence. Their education system had allowed them to train everyone faster and easier on how to operate machines, develop equipment, and work together on assembly lines.

Life in Aronia was good. As times and the world economies got bigger and better, the everyday life of the Aronians improved immensely. The Kings, each in their own time, had homes built for every family. Their homes were kept close to their place of employment with the purpose that they would not have to walk great distances. The Kings kept them employed by staying on top of world demand, science, technology, and by building industries to supply the world and their own people with what was current and needed. The Kings kept the Aronians educated in such a way, that as the demand in certain fields increased, there was always someone educated and ready to fill the niche. The

Kings sent the people abroad to learn methods, technologies and sciences, and involved them in setting up their own industries, as well as teaching others. The Kings made sure that every Aronian knew his worth and instilled in each one the knowledge that without them, Aronia would not be as good a country as it was now, and with their help, Aronia would become a much better place to live in.

Chapter II

King Dominique IV

By A.D. 1987, Aronia, had undergone some significant changes. When the Aronians had entered the Industrial Age they held no favour of holding on to the old, with the exception of the ancient words of "The Great Book". Stone and brick buildings that were once practical were replaced with larger, stronger, glass and steel buildings. Their city was impeccably clean and new with more modern buildings being constantly erected and the old buildings being dismantled. Change was always good. It was moving forward. It was always clean and fresh. Aronians could not understand why other cultures would work so hard, looking backward and spending so much of their resource to cling to past things instead of jumping forward to embrace and create anew. This idealism, as it was written in "The Great Book", had allowed them to survive, grow and prosper.

The lush green forest surrounding the great lake on the Island now had the appearance of a shield guarding the great lake from the enormous skyscrapers and factories that tower over the edge of the forest, looking down on the small trees but not daring to pass their border. This is the city of Trums.

Long sandy beaches seem to be the only thing protecting the ocean from being taken over by this great city. Mammoth skyscrapers tower eighty storeys above the streets. Their only envy is the great volcano, Oden. These immense structures travelled down the coast to the natural harbour which is now bursting with large cargo ships, massive brightly coloured boom cranes, enormous ship yards, and factories. The city glimmers of modern glass and chrome. Glass tubular walk-ways connect all the skyscrapers together midway down the buildings forming a highway system of pedestrians on moving sidewalks.

Dominique Olafur IV sat at his antique, hand carved desk running his fingers through his long hair, tugging at the ends more to see if he had any feeling left in his scalp, than to straighten the hair. Surrounded by piles of papers, books, and dockets, he was almost lost from sight. He felt that the stacks seemed to be leaning inward towards him, and about ready to cause an avalanche that would bury him. It was an analogy befitting his situation.

The room was not extravagant. It was modern and practical. The desk was the only antique in the room. The walls glowed from monitors and televisions built into the wall, adding streams of soft light to the dimly lit room. Another monitor sat on the desk illuminating Dominique's face which had the look of a man who was lost and in need of a map; not to find where he was going, but to find where he was at. He looked tired, stressed and frustrated.

Dominique, the eldest of a family of twelve and reigning King of Aronia, was the final answer to all questions of state. With ministries, boards, regional departmental government, and advisory panels Dominique had all the tools that he needed to help him govern his people but the final decision, right or wrong, was his. All the responsibility was on his head, not the heads of his people. The Olafur Reign had lasted for over four hundred years with peace and prosperity for all. They had held their country from foreign aggression with little to no internal discord.

Dominique lived in the royal palace with his wife Queen Vivian and his two sons Erik and Lars. Erik was first in line to succeed the throne. Dominique was sure that his son was well prepared for the job. From the day of his birth, Erik had been groomed as Dominique had been taught, in order to take on the responsibilities of his people. Looking back on the day, at the stacks of papers and documents to be reviewed and signed, and at the wall covered in large screen monitors with graphs, statistics and historical data from other countries that he had considered worthwhile study to help in his dilemma, Dominique felt it was a job that he would not wish on anyone right now, especially, not on his son.

King Dominique's day had started off early in the morning. He was up at four-thirty for coffee. This gave him time to prepare for what was about to confront him at the Urban Development Board meeting. He had good people, the best of the best, and every department was self-reliant and capable. The King's job was to meld all the departments together to build and make everything work as a whole for the Aronian Society. He had guidance from his brothers and sisters since it was a family affair, and the only job in Aronia that you were born into. Work started the day the soother came out of your mouth. He was to meet with the Royal family over breakfast before the meeting at six A.M. It was a tradition that had been going on for at least a century.

The breakfast was well catered. Fruits, eggs, and coffee were served on the royal silver by the staff members who were dressed in white. "The Great Book" had made it law that no one Aronian was any better than any other. Each person was to earn their position and station by their effort and their contribution. Only the Royal family was the exception to that law. Despite this decree, every Aronian respected and worshipped the Royals. They knew that a Royal's job lasted all day, every day of their lives. This gave the Royals the special status that they received from the people of Aronia.

Dominique greeted his brothers and sisters as he entered the room.

"Good morning Gertrude."

Gertrude was the King's sister who always sat beside him and she was the sibling King Dominique always felt the most at ease with. She was one of the only two sisters in the family. Gertrude was eight years older than her sister was, which made her the only source of female perspective that Dominique had while he was growing up. She was his confidante and his support when it came to personal and family matters. Gertrude had studied Medicine and Business and she was the head of the Medical Board in Aronia. She was less interested in the affairs of world politics and domestic governing than the rest of the family. She was most concerned about the health and well-being of the Aronian people.

"Good morning Erik."

Erik sat directly across the table in order to keep Mikkel from sitting there. Erik was the brother whose opinion Dominique valued the most. Erik was practical, insightful, and wise beyond his years. He treated the biggest decisions with the same air and comfort as he would while choosing to put either jam or marmalade on his toast, which was the dilemma that seemed to be his current problem. Erik was in charge of technologies, manufacturing, and domestic affairs. He was the work horse of the family. Dominique felt he gave too large a work load to him, but he knew he could trust Erik to always get it done right.

"Good morning Mikkel."

Mikkel was the twin brother of Leif and the brother who played the devil's advocate. No one in the family challenged Dominique's authority, but Mikkel would push it. Mikkel had leadership qualities as well, and this caused a bit of friction in personalities between the two because Dominique held the position of King. Even though it had caused many heated debates and was the least attractive part of any of these meetings, Dominique knew that Mikkel never held anything back. If Mikkel could come up with an argument against whatever they were discussing, then, so could anyone in Aronia, or the world. Mikkel was intelligent. His words and beliefs were more passionate and more from the heart than from the brain; however, Mikkel always had in mind what was best for his Country. Dominique valued Mikkel's point of view even though he seldom agreed with it. Mikkel's insights worked like a crystal ball showing the fallout and repercussions that could happen over any decision that Dominique made. He was sure that his father had instilled these qualities into Mikkel, in order to give Dominique a full scope of any problem before making any decision. His father also enjoyed watching the two of them argue and would egg them on by agreeing with both sides. Perhaps he was using this as a teaching tool, to show that two opposite answers could both be right. It all depended on how one viewed things and where their personal beliefs lay.

Mikkel was the Minister of the Mining and Resource Committee and the only family member who did not live in the Royal Palace grounds. He flew in by helicopter every morning for the breakfast meetings. Mikkel believed that if he was responsible for mining and the men doing the mining, then he should be on Vinland Island with them. Living surrounded by miners and farmers, suited Mikkel. He felt it made him more like the people than any other of the Royals. Dominique respected Mikkel for this more than he would ever admit to Mikkel's face, but both Gertrude and Erik knew the respect Dominique had for his younger brother.

"Good morning Val."

Val was Dominique's eyes to the world. He was rarely at one of these meetings. He spent three quarters of the year attending banquets and fund raisers around the world. He was charismatic, charming, and witty. He was the face that the King wanted the world to recognize as Aronia. He held all of Dominique's values. Even though Val's life seemed wonderful and care free to most people, Dominique knew that Val did everything with the same work ethic as any Aronian. He kept Aronia in good standing in the world's eyes.

"Good morning Leif."

Leif was Mikkel's twin brother and was the Brain of the family. He had studied History, Political Science and Economics. Leif knew what made every country tick and how they got that way. When a country was having a problem, Lief would usually be able to tell the King why they were in their predicament and how they would most likely solve it as well as how long it would take to do it. He was essential for the Foreign Diplomacy Policy and for imports and exports.

"Good morning Julius."

Julius was Julius. He was very good at sports and he had competed at the Olympics in the 200 metre breast stroke. He enjoyed fishing and surfing. His desire to be part of the family and their duties was admired by his brothers and sisters, but he was not a specialist on anything in particular. Dominique had Julius sit on the Athletic Boards and that satisfied Julius' need to contribute. He did it with integrity.

"Good morning Rolf."

Rolf was the Minister of Finance. He sat on the Boards of the Aronian Central Bank and Import-Export. He monitored the national budget and his word to the King was absolute when it came to finances.

"Good morning Alex."

Alex was the King's eye on energy. Alexander was twenty two-years-old and an expert in the field of energy. His part was pretty easy and his uncle, Prince Borg, was still there helping to run things. Prince Borg was a bit complacent, because he never believed they could use more power than Oden could pump out. Alex, however, wanted energy consumption monitored and equipment made more efficient on a regular basis. Alex closely watched other countries as they started to have problems with energy demands. He wanted to utilize solar and wind turbines in Aronia. His uncle had said it was a waste of time, until Aronia had its first brown out. Alex won the whole family's respect, when in weeks; he had solar panels on the tops of every high-rise in Aronia.

"Good morning Ivar."

Ivar was an architect and worked in the field of engineering and construction. To Ivar, the city of Trums was a pallet and a creation of his work of art. Dominique loved going to Ivar's office. He had models and drawings of his visions of his city in its completion, and it was beautiful. Dominique would purposely comment on something that he would change just to see Ivar have a panic attack.

Vegar and Eir were abroad attending to affairs of state. Vegar was head of the Board of Agriculture and Eir headed the Board of Education. Both had the uncles working beside them because of their young age, but both were fully capable. Eir was the baby sister. All of the Royals treated her special because she was the youngest of the family. All, that is, except Alexander. To him, she was a best friend, as well as, his little sister.

Both the agriculture and the education departments were greatly respected, not only by the Aronians and the Royals, but also by the world. Aronia's education system was the envy of the world. Every Aronian attended school. No one had to pay for their education and it involved the actual participation of the students in their chosen field once they turned twelve years of age.

Agriculture was Aronia's other world stage. Their lack of space forced Aronia to get creative with their farming methods. They started planting crops vertically, using large tubes planted in the earth. They filled the tubes with fertile soil and planted the seeds in pockets up the sides. Fertilizer and water was added in perfect amounts at the top of the tube and the seeds would grow from the pockets on the sides, creating trees out of ground crops. This increased the yields several times over; it also made harvesting an easy mechanized job with no damage to the produce.

After saying the good mornings, Dominique got right down to business.

"This morning's issue is going to be the one that no one wants to confront. Today is our Urban Development Board meeting and the topics are the same as before: no more room to develop straight out. I think Ivar has given me the numbers which tell us that expansion in Trums can only accommodate the population growth for two more years. He has some suggestions that he will fill us in on, but agriculture is having a simulator problem with demand which outweighs the land on which we have to produce, on both Vinland and Tors Islands. Vegar has sent me his report since he is not here and it shows that exports are dropping because of the rise in domestic demand. We are running out of room folks, and I am not hearing any answers."

Rolf replied. "The issue of supply of our agricultural exports is self-levelling. We raise our price until demand reaches the supply. That's economics. With the sugar cane, we have too much competition; but, with kiwi and other exotic fruits and vegetables, our supply will direct world prices. Vegar will have to assess the crops and their availability on the world market. By using the world price, he will then have to determine how to best use the land we do have. I realize that is just a patch, but it should help out. I will discuss it further with Vegar when he returns home."

"Thank you, Rolf," said Dominique. "Getting the most for what we have is all we can do now, but we have to look at twenty and fifty years down the road as well."

Ivar addressed the table. "Engineering has come up with some off shore engineering plans to build right over the water and they look pretty sound. There is a twenty-four square kilometres land mass sitting five metres beneath the surface of the ocean that we can build on. We have the technology which would change very little. The exception is the construction methods we use and we are on top of that. We can build right over the ocean with the foundations working as pillars so that the water flows well under the structure. We are conducting core samples of the ocean floor, but we believe that, geologically speaking, the rock formations will be the same as the mainland itself. Volcanic rock is volcanic rock and it works very well in supporting the sub structure of a skyscraper. Transport would be the same with moving sidewalks on the twentieth floor. Connection to the mainland is a bit more difficult. We are looking at bridging and a monorail system, but right now, the best our technology can get us is a cable car system."

Ivar carried on. "We can build on Oden's finger, right out to the lighthouse. It's easier, but it only gives us three square kilometres. The advantage is that it connects to the main land, so there will be less transportation problems. There are teams in place to test the sub Atlantic plate and rock structure to ascertain what kind of load it can bear, but they are pretty sure that with our technology, and the premise that it's all the same volcanic rock, eighty stories is still possible. Our figures show that at the current birth rate of three and a half million per year and the death rate of three hundred and twenty-five thousand per year, Oden's finger would sustain housing for three years. By that time we should have the off shore housing underway. Twenty-four square kilometres would last fifteen years at the current population growth, but our percentage growth works on a curve and in using that figure, we would only be able to supply housing for sixteen years tops, even with including the off shore development."

"Thank you Ivar. Any questions?" asked Dominique. "Well then, let us allow Ivar to go and set up for today's board meeting, if you are done your breakfast, Ivar." Dominique turned towards Ivar and said: "I look forward to seeing the drawings of your vision of the off shore concept and your models, Ivar. We will see you in a couple of hours."

Ivar nodded and quietly left the table to prepare for the meeting.

Dominique's head dropped and he grasped his hair. "What are we are going to do in twenty more years. What will we do then?" Dominique asked. "The problem is us. We are over populating!"

Dominique scanned everyone's eyes as he said this, but his head turned to face Mikkel before Mikkel had even uttered a word.

"The Great Book," Mikkel exclaimed.

"The Great Book" written in the sixteenth century by Dominique's ancient forefather, King Domi Olafur I, was held and known as the only religion that the Aronians knew. King Domi I had rid the country of the Spanish and their ideas. He had united the whole of Aronia under the idealism of practicality and education. Gone were the beliefs in Gods controlling crops, weather, and good or bad fortune. The job of all was to take care of their own, strive for excellence in everything they did, and let no one strike fear or discontent into the hearts of others. The list was long and most certainly a wonderful way to run a society. It was the best way, as far as Dominique was concerned. To go against King Domi's commandments was political suicide. It was the one thing that Dominique knew would cause an internal struggle in his country, but he was running out of options. If King Domi I had known of the social implications of one of lines of "The Great Book", he would have clearly added and stated something like, "Until our enemies, from across the sea subside and disease is cured." The line in "The Great Book" read: *"Be fruitful and give this earth as many children as you have food to feed and shelter to keep, for an Aronian is the greatest gift you have to offer, and your stature shall surely grow with each Aronian you set forth upon this earth."* Dominique understood King Domi's reasoning. He had almost lost the Island because their population was too low to supply soldiers to fight the Spanish, but in today's world, it had caused an overpopulation problem.

"'The Great Book' does account for this." Mikkel continued. "'Food to feed and shelter to keep' and I agree with you that we are coming to that point. Other countries have controls on breeding and so do we by an Aronian's station in life. We need to just lower the number of children per station until the population balances out.

So much for my crystal ball, thought Dominique; but, it was obvious to Dominique that Mikkel had been trouble shooting this question as long as he had, and it seemed that Mikkel was unable to come up with no other answers. That was a good sign, Dominique thought; however, he had been hoping that Mikkel would have had something up his sleeve that he, himself, had not thought of to fix the problem.

"But that's not how the people will see it," Leif pointed out. "They all work and have large enough incomes to have as many children as they are allowed by their stations. Our economy is growing, both in exports and domestic usage. Not everyone will understand, they are building

Aronia and making it better. It will cause a division, not only between them and the government, but between the people themselves. It strikes at the equality values as well. 'Why did my father get to have more children than I, when I have accomplished the same or more,' will be asked by the people. We know our grandfather put controls on child birth, by lowering them, and that caused the Crown to go to our father way before his time."

"I think the people of Aronia are flexible enough and knowledgeable enough to accept the situation and work towards an answer, Leif," replied Gertrude.

Leif would play devil's advocate, today, thought Dominique.

"It's instilled in them though, Gertrude." Leif explained. "Having more children is their contribution, their birth right, and their bit of history. I know Dominique has led by example by only having two children, and I know that is why he has done this, but the people of Aronia are still bothered by the fact their King has only two to ascend the throne. If their belief is strong enough, they will not see the facts as we see them. They will see the side of the equation that allows them to continue on with their traditions, our traditions."

Dominique gave Gertrude a look of shock.

"Don't look at me that way, I never told him that is why you only had two children. Leif figured that out all on his own," she retorted.

Val looked puzzled. He turned towards Dominique. "What if we decreed five children per couple and they had five daughters. They would want a son or vice versa. You know this. Vivian would kill for a daughter."

"It will affect productivity, as well as the genetic development of the Island, if everyone is allowed two children. The genetically superior and genetically inferior would then populate at the same rate causing the national average to decrease intellectually. The motivation to succeed decreases as well, because there is no reward for over achieving," Leif added.

"Okay!" Dominique said forcefully. "I have already accepted that they will not look fondly upon me over this. Many will hate me, but unless you have an alternative, Val, what can we do? I need everyone's head on this. I want complete secrecy until we figure out how to ease into this and educate the people so that they can draw to the same conclusion as we have. It is either that or you come up with a better suggestion. We need a half million new housing units in the next year. That's what they are going to tell us at this meeting. That may be doable, but next year, we will need five hundred and fifty thousand and so on."

"The housing maybe doable, but the energy is not." Alexander added. "The natural resources are getting thin. Geothermal will only get us so far. We have always known that the pressure from Oden was up and down, not consistent. We cannot fuel all the new buildings and factories. We are going to have to use fossil fuel generation very soon to keep up with the demand, especially if the world comes out of this recession. Solar is going on everything, so we have some time there, but there will come a point that solar will take care of housing, but not any expansion in industry. Sorry, King, but that's the facts. I did not want to put anything more on your plate, but I thought you should know. If we can improve solar technology and put wind generation on barges, we may be able to hold off the fossil fuels."

"Thank you, Alexander. I need to know all the facts, but I am confident that you find a solution other than fossil fuels. I will give you anybody you need to help with the solar programme."

"Anyone else?" asked Dominique, who was exhausted. "Okay. Everyone put your minds and your focus on this and I am sure we will figure it all out in time. Let's adjourn to the board meeting."

The meeting was exactly what Dominique had expected. The proposal to develop Oden's finger, a point that went out about a mile into the sea and had done nothing but wreak havoc on unsuspecting ships, was passed, and now, here he was in his office trying to find an answer that would appease his people and fix the problem. Dominique's mind was flooded with questions. What should the number be? Would it change if you had all boys or all girls? What if a child dies? Do you get to replace him or her? What if you have a child after you have reached your limit? Do you punish them? Accidents happen. What if you have twins for your last child? Is it like winning a bonus round?

Dominique's father, Lars II, knew that the prosperity of Aronia was not without its costs. King Lars' father had stepped down and given him the crown when Lars was only twenty-two years old. King Lars' battle was to get the people to accept his father's changes in the number of children they could have. It took most of his reign. King Lars' contribution to Aronia was much like King Domi II, negotiating trade while the rest of the world was split and choosing sides. Aronia's position was awkward because many viewed their system the same as communism or a dictatorship. Dominique's father was a negotiator and a diplomatic genius at navigating through tough spots and always came out looking like the good guy without selling himself to either side of the conflict. His bad health and early death made Dominique King at twenty-five years of age.

Aronia, being one of the world's engineering capitals and the most innovative agricultural mecca, had grown up and up and up. Not only was Trums the tallest city in the world with engineering feats of skyscrapers and transportation, but the fields of agriculture and energy were the best in the world with the most innovative concepts. The city, Trums, was almost completely fuelled by Oden, the great volcano, that hundreds of centuries ago likely was the creator of the small country. The Industrial Age was Dominique's great, great, great grandfather's dilemma. To Dominique, now, it looked like a walk in the park. Pollution was quickly resolved by Dominique III as the volcano's destructive power that threatened to destroy, was changed into an industrial advantage that was unmatched by anyone in the world. It created nearly free unlimited power for the Island. It was an engineering feat that was unrivalled in the nineteenth century.

Every generation of Olafur's had a dilemma that looked impossible to solve. Of that I am sure; and every Olafur has arrived at an answer that has made the country stronger, thought Dominique. How I need to draw from their insights, and their visions to help me make any decisions that I decide on. Dominique poured another glass of Aronian scotch for himself, and then, laid his head on the desk to try to find his vision.

Chapter III

The Erikson Family

The Eriksons were your average Aronian family living and working in the city of Trums. This evening Peder was sitting in his chair reading his paper studying the section on world events as Margot, his wife, finishes packing lunches for him and the children for tomorrow.

"Don't pack me so much for tomorrow, they're giving a lunch during the conference, give mine to Nikkulai he's far too skinny." Peder said.

"Would you like an espresso or a coffee?" Margot asked.

Peder jumps up from his chair "No let me get it" Peder said

"Already got it would you settle. What would you like?" Margot asked

"Coffee if it's ready but don't go making a pot for me" replied Peder

Margot walked in the living room.

"Already did Hun" she said.

Peder gets up to help his wife sit in the recliner; she's eight months pregnant with her seventh child. Sitting back Margot said, "Nikkulai's lunch is already big enough for three kids twice his size, I don't know where he puts it all!" Oh and Children got there grades Today."

"And?" Replies Peder.

Margot sips her tea knowing its killing Peder waiting to hear the marks "they're okay."

"OK! Why? Who is slacking?" Peder's voice is hurt and concerned a sense of worry running through his eyes.

"My god Peder you'd think one of the children just died, their marks are terrific. Just settle down." Margot starts giggling to herself as she sips her tea knowing Peder's anxiety is building.

"I swear you're more nervous waiting for their marks than they are, except for Octavious he really wants to be a doctor" she giggled.

"How'd he do?" Peder asked.

"Octavious is at university levels in all his classes school has opened his options slightly and he's overjoyed that they will offer him extra sciences." Margot explained, "And Mary is University advanced levels in all her classes, school has given her her pick and she's leaning towards business like her Dad. Olaf is a mix of both, but they are suggesting he work toward engineering because of his math and would like us to start edging him towards that. Svein has to take two catch up courses in his mathematics but his languages are impressive they want him to pursue an academic writing course and seminars this yr. Nikkulai has above average grades. His leadership skills and organization skills are in the top of the class and his grade three aptitude test said he is mechanical by nature and likes to build, they have given us some ideas of toys and books that may help. Tor is above average I.Q with a fondness for computers, his reading, writing, and arithmetic are all within school standards."

Peder obviously overjoyed by the grades said "Well I'll bet you had a smile on your face with Tor's report, taking after his Mom. Computers are the wave of the future; they will make everything easier and faster. The course I'm taking on computer business applications is a breeze thanks to your help."

"It's Nice. Computer sciences are a great career. Look at me I can still actively pursue my career take care of you and the kids all from home," Margot said.

"Well don't push it too much Hun, they told you do what you can to help out, family first," Peder stressed.

"If Mary wants business I'd tell her to do some of Nikkulai's leadership courses as well," Peder said.

"Why's that?" asked Margot.

"My leadership training is one of my biggest assets at work," Peder told her.

"I'm sure your people would be lost without your leadership," Margot giggled.

"Got a great team behind me at work but trying to keep them all on the same page at the same time is the trick. They're starting to doubt me from time to time now because we keep running out of parts. It's not so much quotas being up as it is getting the steel parts; the supply is getting slower and slower. Our steel mills have to depend on the foreign ore, getting it on time, and filling everyone's needs in Aronia."

"I tell the govern that we can't depend on foreign ore. We should get control over the mines to keep production up, we need to buy the mines abroad and run them ourselves to keep production up. The rest of the world would just have the hard case built abroad and shipped here but the board would flip if I suggested that. Since the domestic mines have all but dried up or at least can't keep up with demand, the domestic demand for; laptops , V.C.R's and CD players keeps rising my charts say I won't be able to keep up with foreign orders by next year unless we get a consistent flow of steel frames."

"Does the board know this?" Margot asked.

"They know the problem but Jonas keeps bragging about his ten kids more than discussing the problems, His eldest has been selected for the presidents' conference in July and his other son the world leadership conference next week." Peder said, a little perturbed because he had been due for a promotion to Jonas's position for a long time.

"Can you convey the problem over his head and get it to the governance committee?" Margot asked.

"Yes, my month end report goes to the governance board and they have to get back to me with a solid answer of which directions are suitable for Aronian national policy and the betterment of the nation. Our problems lie with our supplier of raw materials which is out of our control and Jonas has done everything in search of a solid supply he can here in Aronia. Having Aronia buy up foreign mines was my suggestion," Peder shrugged.

Peder goes back to his paper Margot goes to her computer to finish off some programming before bed.

"See here the United Nations is complaining about Aronia's immigration policies or the lack thereof. They are calling us a socialist based society ruled by an absolute Monarchy. They say here that we are taking advantage of world trade and world economics but we are still unwilling to open immigration policies to allow immigrants into Aronia. Have they ever been to Aronia? Immigrants, we don't even have enough room for all our own Aronians let alone let in someone else. At the beach last Sunday if one more person had of shown up one would have had to be pushed into the ocean." The statement turned inadvertently into an image in Peder's mind. He envisioned people being set in the middle of an island by a giant hand and every time you add one to the center an outside ring of people slide into the ocean.

"Well I don't know Peder; we do lack the ethnic diversity of other nations because of our traditions and laws. I thought it was a nice change last year when we went to the United States on that business trip. It made me feel more worldly just standing in one place."

"Ethnic diversity" he sneered "we had enough ethnic diversity back when the Spanish immigrated to Aronia, I mean in all those countries whoever is allowed to follow whatever religion they want. Our Great Book says straight out that 'no one but Aronian blood shall prosper over Aronian soil,' that is our religion so why won't they respect our beliefs. Besides have we ever had a civil War in Aronia?" Peder asked.

Margot leaned back from the computer rubbing her stomach, "no not since the great book was written at least but I think it's more about the fact that we have the policy than the fact that we wouldn't actually have room to put them. Our country's very prosperous and other's want a piece of that and we have a great life. If you lived somewhere else wouldn't you want to move your family here?" Margot asked.

"Of course I would but if that option wasn't open wouldn't I just work harder to make the place I was born better. The Royal Family's Job has been made much easier because there people all have the same beliefs and goals, so we all work together towards the same thing. Can you imagine what other nations leaders have to deal with, they have twenty different religions and cultures that all believed that it is there job to convert every one too their faith and traditions. They all want different things and they are insulted when others don't follow their traditions, I don`t envy those countries. That's why they all have to import there goods from us, they can`t get anything done in all the chaos," Peder gave a smirk and gave Margot a kiss.

"It has worked well for Aronia, but that has a lot to do with the fact we are an island hundreds of miles from anyone else. No one is inadvertently walking here and building a house or a church," Margot said.

"Hahaha true" said Peder, "never thought of that. Guess being an island has given us a bit of an advantage. Good and bad, cup half full half empty." He set the paper down walked over and kissed Maggot passionately like they were still young love then bends over and kisses her stomach. Peder headed out on the patio looking down sixty seven floors to the streets below. "No smog, no traffic, no crime, no wars, yah we ought to follow their example it's working so well for them," Peder exclaimed to the open space sarcastically.

Peder had done well for himself, he had realized his successes thus far but felt he could do more and wanted to move up in his career so he would be able to accomplish more. After hearing his children's marks and watching them grow, full of drive and determination at such young ages Peder felt the pride that only children bring you. Peder was sure that He and Margot had to list the raising of their children as their greatest success.

Where Peder felt the longing to contribute most was getting his idea's heard and implemented in other sectors and he would have liked to have seen them take an interest in him at a Government level, but that wasn't in his schooling. His problem solving skills had been his biggest asset his whole life, his knack for business and leadership helped his problem solving get implementation. The Aronian education system as well had picked up on Peder's abilities quickly and moved him towards a career in business start-up, operations set up, and production improvement because they saw the world economy coming and realized the need for people like Peder.

Peder's ability to quickly adapt and understand the functions of all the divisions and the ability to see the best utilization of each division and each person working in those divisions moved him up the corporate ladder fast. Peder would see the limits of each worker and each piece of equipment within a couple of minutes of viewing either. This soon gave Peder the top production numbers in the industry and he was given training to move up even higher but there were no available position for quite a while.

Because of this Peder had been in an eight bedroom for a while now and in a month he would be filling his last bedroom. He and Margot had been to the doctor and the doctor said the baby would be a boy, and was perfectly healthy. Peder could see Margot had forced the smile when the doctor told them and he himself had been hoping for a daughter. Peder enjoyed raising his daughter, she was daddy's little girl which is probably why Margot wanted a girl so she could pretty her up and make her more mom's girl this time.

Children were the seeds to building a society and opening up the future, every Aronian new the quote from the great book but Peder truly understood it. Peder always considered King Domi as wise way before his time, everything in the Great Book may appear as common sense now but in King Domi's time it would have been an act of genius. Peder knew that what Domi envisioned was a society that would continue to grow wiser smarter and stronger. What Domi was creating by making his laws was for everyone to supply sons and daughters that where smarter stronger and more driven than they themselves where and they with their children. By doing this the country would become stronger and greater every generation. Peder realised that the opposite was true as well, if a generation allows their children to be lazy, weak, without direction or drive the cycle would work in reverse planting seeds of decaying and destruction in the society that they inhabit.

Peder was worried however about whether the system could hold up and felt that it may break down before the end of his life time. Each generation's duty was to make Aronia better for the next generation, to help the country grow and prosper. Each generation was supposed to make the world a better place to live, for the next generation and so on, but Aronia was an Island that was already developed beyond anyone's dreams or expectations and it had cost Aronia most of their natural resources to do it. The problem as far as Peder saw it, was that his children had no place to make Aronia grow, nowhere to build anything bigger or better, just no room. His children where ambitious, smart and full of creativity and if he hands them a world where they are not allowed to use those gifts they would become bitter, become lazy, lose their drive and their children would be worse. He felt that his children would be blamed for the cycle that destroys Aronia, but it would be his generations fault.

Peder would often think of a floating island with fields and floating cities, with the vision beautiful and vibrant in his mind he would think to himself my children are in that city designing and building the next Island. Peder had to think this and he knew the vision was force and contrived to make him feel better because not thinking it was possible was too depressing to bear.

Peder had faith in the King and the Royal family, the Royals had always been the ones who could find the solution. King Dominique the fourth was a very young King but he was super intelligent and as honourable a King as Aronia had ever known. King Lars the third had trained his son well; it was almost as if he knew he would pass early in life. King Lars himself was given the throne young in his life because his father felt the disfavour of the Aronian people and chose to give them a new King instead of letting the contempt fester.

King Erik the third, King Dominique's grandfather, felt that with the advent of modern medicine and with no wars striking there island that the population would explode and they would not have enough food or room for all the people. He explained the problem to the people, raised the age of consensual Marriage to twenty three and made mandatory schooling up until that age. This he felt would take three years away from the people reproducing. He then raised the qualifying levels set by ones station on the size ones family could be. The top achievers would now be allowed ten instead of twelve children and anyone who was a labourer would only be allowed two children but would always have the right and the opportunity to advance. He felt by doing this that it would make Aronians work harder and have more drive to succeed therefor improving Aronia as a whole. That would be the end of King Erik the III as he would hand the crown to his son King Lars, Dominique's father, to stop any anarchy within his people.

This may of actually worked and it bought some time, Peder thought, but Aronians did work harder and there drive did improve even more than it had been and soon all of the advanced Aronians where over qualified and had nowhere to advance. At that time world economies where growing very fast and the Aronians started markets and businesses faster than any, opening up new top position with every new market and with that the ability for more people to reach positions that allowed them to have up to ten children.

Peder was sure that the King would only lower the limits on the amount of children as a last resort in lute of this history but he was afraid for his children's sake that the King may have little choice. Peder also felt that under a situation where no one could have large families with less competition and lower benefits for succeeding the cycle of deterioration to the society would be even more severe.

No matter how intelligent Peder was the relevance of his own family and his contribution to the situation never entered his mind. The social problem of overpopulation did not related in his mind as too many people, it was just that the Island was too small. From birth Peder had always known that the measure of one's stature and success was by the size of one's family. Too reach ten children was the goal of every Aronian and an honour only achieved by the most gifted. It had been the case from the time King Domi had written the great book and it had been the measuring stick of every generation since.

Chapter IV

OH CANADA

Brian was happy to have a job. His divorce had cost him everything he had worked his whole life to build. The marriage had been relatively successfully for his ex-wife Shannon, she had all her debts paid during the marriage, she got money for a house that she had no money into, all new furniture and when the house went through foreclosure she had no responsibility for the fifty thousand dollars that some lawyer had paid himself to fill in the blanks and signing his name.

Brian had been laid off when it all went down. Ten days after he paid his ex-wife twenty thousand dollars on her share of the house and they had filled out the paperwork at the mortgage company, the mortgage company called in the mortgage even though he had never missed a mortgage payment, thirty days later they filed for foreclosure. A house that was paid down to sixty five thousand dollars left owing was now one hundred and fifteen thousand dollars in debt. Brian sold the house quickly and was left owing twenty thousand.

Brian had an above average I.Q as a matter of fact he was in the top two percent in Canada. He had some college experience but finances and the realization that there was no design jobs for when he finished the course made him drop out before getting his degree. He went back to get the prerequisites he would need to be able to apply for university, to keep his options open, planning to go back for university at a later date. He would have liked business or teaching history, politics and economics were his passion but he did not hold a lot of respect for politicians and he would take economics if he went through for business anyway. That would have been what he liked, what he got was a job. To survive Brian had to use the only asset anyone seemed to appreciate, a strong back, and the best paying jobs at the time were hard labour positions at twelve dollars an hour. Brian seldom admitted to it but he enjoyed hard physical labour, the feel of his muscles being stretch to the limit. Brian had found if he didn't work out or do something physical during the day, to use up all that energy, he couldn't sleep at night.

Shortly after that he got married to Shannon his girlfriend of three years, he bought the three story red brick home that was a wreck and fixed it up himself. He had bought the house for ninety thousand and by doing all the work himself had made it a beautiful Victorian home just in time to lose it. It was appraised at one hundred and twenty one thousand dollars for the divorce, and after proving all the down payment had been made by him and she supplied nothing to the relationship the judge only allotted Shannon twenty thousand. As soon as he had paid her, that's when the mortgage company called in the mortgage.

Brian moved into a boarding house, it was a small white sided home with six bedrooms a bathroom a kitchen and a living room; it was run by a large native Canadian woman named Ruth whose sense of humour was only out done by her temper when her bottle of whiskey ran out. Brian was able to get along with her, he actually enjoyed her company, and he personally never had a falling out with her, but he had to break up a couple fights where she had beaten the crap out of one of the guys.

He didn't mind living in the boarding house, it was cheap; it was somewhere to cook, sleep and read his books, when he had time. He got a second job cleaning a local bar at two hundred dollars a week plus was working lots of overtime. He was working nineteen hours a day so he didn't spent much time at the boarding house anyhow and any spare time he spent with his friends usually at the Coffee Pub.

Brian's main source of income came from Pre Fab Concrete Structures a company that produced pre-fabricated concrete parking garages, water treatment plants and bridges. The work was hard and heavy but the foremen where good and the conversation and camaraderie with his co-workers made it tolerable.

The highlights of the days at work where lunch hours when he and his fellow employees would talk about world affairs, political, social, economic, Canadian politics and even religion if it wasn't too serious. The conversation was pretty one sided, the guys were not nearly as well versed or studied as Brian but they would bring up some good arguments and some meaningful solutions . Brian would know facts, percentages and the history behind almost any claim. He could do complex math in his head in seconds and the guys he worked with knew Brian could not go through life not knowing an answer to a question. If they could find something that Brian didn't know the answer to, they knew it would drive him crazy and he would have to go to the library and study the subject till he did. This was a game they liked to play on him though it was rare to be able to find anything to stump him.

Brian would joke at the end of lunch "well damn I think we solved all of Canada's problems today, tomorrow let's see if we can fix the middle east," and it was just a joke because no one would ever bring up the middle east while Brian was around. He had read every book on the subject and would visit anyone from town who had just recently visited there. Iraq was his favourite country in the world and the city of Ur was the one place he most wanted to visit. The birth place of civilization.

Brian's real pleasure came when he had time on the weekends to sit in the coffee shop and talk; politics, social issues economics, the stock market and girls with his friends Jason and John. Here the conversations would dive deeper into the problems and many of the solutions they would come up with were a damn site better than the ones the government would. Brian would often write the government or go see his M.P with some of these ideas in hopes someone would catch on, but it never happened.

Jason was the owner of the Coffee Pub, a local coffee franchise that served up- scale coffee and decent food. He was a yuppie; he had short brown spikey hair always in the fashion of the latest television show. He was slightly chunky and worn fashionable attire from the same television shows that he had chosen his hair cut. He had worked his way through business school and then struggled hard to get his family to buy him a coffee franchise. He like the role of the young big shot business man which Brian and John teased him about and made fun of him behind his back. Jason was not Brian's idea of a self-made hundredaire but he was a nice guy with a clue and a sense of humour which wasn't that easy to find.

John on the other hand was what he appeared, not so yuppyish, had earned every penny he ever had, and probably still had it, but didn't really like working so much. John had sandy hair and a baby face that most considered honest. He dressed very much in the same yuppie fashion as Jason but his presentation and the appearance of being successful wasn't as important to him. He was in good shape and stayed active in sports but wasn't big into hitting the weights. John had retired at twenty nine years of age and made a living off of the stock market. John had more than a clue; he was Brian's equal and was the only worthwhile debate or intense conversation Brian had. This in Brian's opinion is what made them such strong friends, if it wasn't for Brian's intellect John wouldn't have put up with Brian either.

Brian wasn't like John and Jason when it came to appearance. Where they opted for fashionable conformity Brian just didn't care. What people thought of the way he looked or acted met nothing to him, he considered their opinion no more of a concern than that of an ant or a fly that he was about to swat. Brian had long curly blonde hair that he rarely combed. His attire was whatever he had on when he left home or work. He felt that if other people had a problem with his work cloths it was probably because they had never done a hard day's work so why would he care what they think. He had penetrating blue eyes that seemed to be able to stare into people's souls. Brian was in top physical shape constantly working out and had the physique of a novice body builder. All three where attractive and none had any problems with getting those of the opposite sex to look their way.

Brian had just paid off all his debts and saved up enough to buy an old junker of a car. He fixed it so it was road worthy and had just enough to pay the insurance and buy Christmas presents. When he got to the Coffee Pub the conversation was going to be about Christmas shopping, because Brian came in the Coffee Pub ranting.

"There is not one damn thing in any of these stores that's made in this country," he ranted.

"And how are you today," Jason laughed getting him his coffee.

"Did you know that the only doll you can buy that's made in Canada is a porcelain collectable doll for nine hundred dollars in New Hamburge?"

"No I didn't know that, out Christmas shopping I take it," Jason remarked.

"He won't buy anything unless it's made in Canada for anyone at Christmas. We get this conversation every year," said John who has been friends with Brian since high school and had heard Brian rant about this every year.

"Yah but every year I found at least something decent for everybody, this year I couldn't find anything, it's all made in Aronia," Brian said wanting at least someone to be upset with him.

Jason explained "its economics, wages are too high in Canada along with taxes, workman compensation rates and insurance."

Jason, being a small business owner that was labour intensive and highly competitive, would always focus on wages. Even with coffees high margins it took a lot of one dollar coffee's to have a high enough gross to cover the overheads.

Brian snaps back at Jason "Germany's wages are higher, and their country does quite well and their people have more vacation time and better benefits. The Germans also concentrate on keeping production and production jobs in Germany. Canadians are under paid if anything, we can hardly get ahead now and you are suggesting that we should take a pay cut so corporate Canada can compete with Aronia? It's absurd. It's capitalists with a complete lack of economic sense is what it is. These capitalists take and take and never give back, that's how they make their profits today. These idiots don't have the brain power to know that if they move all the manufacturing jobs to Aronia there will not be any North Americans left to buy their products. It's the Government's fault as well, but both Canada and the United States governments are owned by capitalist interests anyway. The government needs to stop taking tariffs off any country that's not on the same playing field as Canada. Free trade only works with similar countries with similar governments; they are essentially giving Canada away."

"You can't blame a business man for taking a product that costs him five dollars an hour to produce in Canada and outsourcing it to Aronia were he can have the product made for two dollars an hour," said Jason, baffled as to how Brian can't see the business sense in that.

"I most certainly can blame the business man and my Government for allowing that business man to be an economical buffoon. To save this moron from himself the government needs to put a tariff of three dollars on the product coming from Aronia, or they could just re-evaluate the Aronian currency to what it should be," Brian said.

"Brian that's protectionism," John injected "But I agree with the re-evaluating of the Aronian currency, that would probably even things out anyway."

"That's how the United States became the world power they exported everything to every country tariff free and tariffed everything coming into their country." Brian said.

"Then buy a Coffee Pub basket it's made in Canada." Jason joked hoping to end the conversation.

"Ok" Brian said "I'll take six of them as long as everything in it is made in Canada, but if there's anything in it that's not made in Canada I get them for free."

Jason looked at Brian and started laughing, then he looks at John and said "shit I don't know. "

"Bet? " Brian said "I'll pay double and buy a round if it's all made in Canada."

Jason was laughing but Brian knew it was too buy time while he was thinking "No, I can't do it, I don't know where the basket came from, it's probably Aronian, Sarah bought them and she probably went to the dollar store."

"I don't care what store she got the basket in; you ain't growing coffee in Canada." Brian said with a condescending snicker.

Jason and John started laughing there asses off as Jason hit himself on the forehead and said. "You know if I had of known the baskets were from Canada I'd of taken that stupid bet, ass hole."
Brian laughed at him then goes right back to ranting.

"Listen this doesn't work if all our manufacturing is sent down to Aronia don't these morons realizes the economic inevitability is that they won't have any one who can buy their product but Aronians and they already make their own."

"You make too much out of this stuff Brian. They are menial labour jobs that don't mean anything, so a bunch of women who wove basket in Canada lost their job, they can get another one working at a burger joint that pays the same "Jason said laughing at him.

"John, would you like to explain to business school Jason the difference between working at a burger joint and weaving baskets here in Canada." Brian said in that condescending voice.

Jason was still laughing at Brian until the snide business school Jason remark came up, looked at John.

"I don't know what he's talking about, he probably means the service industry verses the manufacturing industry." John said on the hook for an answer.

"And why does that make a difference John?" Brian said not letting John off the hook yet.

"It doesn't," Jason said.

"It most certainly does Jason!" Brian exclaimed horrified "do you not understand the difference? If everyone in the country worked in the service industry, who would we service?"

"Each other I guess," laughed Jason.

"Ok, cause this is a real problem, firemen, cops, judges are all great jobs, nothing but respect for the guys who do it right, government employees not so much respect, but all have a net worth to Canada of zero, they create nothing they add no value to your county or the world whatsoever. They are born, they do their job, they die, nothing added, you can argue the fire fighter may have preserved something of a tangible value I'll accept that, but the cops and the government employees left nothing no sign that they've ever been here at all." Brian said looking like he's standing there giving a lecture but Jason's a bit offended feeling like Brian is making him out to be stupid and Jason doesn't like that.

Jason objected "You can't say that, what if the cop saves a life."

"Well you can argue that, if he saved the life of a basket weaver, but if he saves the life of another cop or a fast food employee, double negative, government employee triple negative."

Brian laughed and John tells him he's terrible and then goes on to explain.

"What Brian is talking about is true gross domestic product G.D.P. Many obviously Brian and I have to agree somewhat, won't accept these new G.D.P numbers. Real G.D.P. does mean that you must have created something that didn't exist before, to have anything worth a tangible value or add to your G.D.P." John explained "Service industry does help that existence work better by ideally selling Canadian manufactured goods but the bureaucracy is the thing that is growing and as Brian is trying to prove adds little to a country."

"OK well I created a business" — said Jason

"Yes and your dollars went to someone who made the coffee maker, built this building and the guy who grows the produce you use. So you contributed to someone who contributes to the GDP but you yourself do not. Brian said with the insinuation that the people that Jason obviously looked down at where the ones he should be looking up to.

"Don't Jason he's just up on himself because he is the only one that fits the criteria of someone who contributes to the country's G.D.P," John said saving Jason the effort of arguing and not wanting to allow any more fuel for Brian's fire. "If everyone was a service industry worker the only money would come from the central bank and it would have no backing at all because the country printing it would have nothing to back it with. Of course if everyone worked in the service industry there would be nothing to serve, we wouldn't have houses to live in either." John said covering both Brian's points.

"Don't worry Aronia will ship us houses don't know how we'll get them here from the docks though," Brian laughed. "But it brings me to a very important point how can fifty percent of the country's population who work and contributing to the GDP afford to pay fifty percent of the population that doesn't, and the people like the police, Firefighter, teachers, and the government employees get paid more than the people paying them?"

"I thought we were talking about Christmas present," Jason said not really grasping the new subject and wondering how they had gotten to this point from discussing Christmas presents.

"We are that's what I'm saying we are sending all the real jobs to Aronia, they are playing a paper game keeping their currency low so the labour's cheaper but they have all the best technology and no debt, how does that work?" Brian said easing off Jason a little.

"They're paid less than anywhere," Jason answered.

"No shit why do they get paid at all, they get free housing, free food, free transit, free education, free dental, Hell I get paid what everyone keeps telling me is a good wage and I can't afford those things and then they get blow money on top of it," Brian said a little upset that he's always broke.

"You don't know that," Jason said "they say they're getting that stuff maybe but we don't know."

Brian agreed saying "They say we have the highest standard of living, so you're right either they don't know shit or the rest of the world's living worse than me, but not Aronians."

"They probably are paid, and buy those things, Brian, they are just paid in notes that aren't accepted by the I.M.F, you need to explain this stuff. I'm not sure and either are you. I know they have free housing, medical and dental but I think they receive a wage for their living expenses, if they leave the country for a vacation or something they exchange their national currency with the Aronian pound, then to whatever currency they need elsewhere," John added.

"Don't you see Jason economically if everything here and the U.S or the rest of the world for that matter is made in Aronia it's not possible for it to be some poor country, because they are creating stuff, adding real GDP to their country, eventually they have everything and all we have is some fancy accounting," Brian explained.

"It happened with Taiwan," John stated. "The United States set up their factories in Taiwan for the cheap labour and the lack of patent law protection, to produce goods with the profits coming back to the United States, you have to remember when everything said made in Taiwan on the bottom."

"Yah even Canadian souvenirs "Jason laughed but you could tell that Jason liked the idea and business sense of what the Americans had done.

John helped reinforce Brian's point "yah well look, Taiwan was the only county in the world that could back their currency in gold in no time. Why? Because there people where making real gross domestic products. As soon as their currency was re-evaluated and traded at what its true value was all the factories left because labour costs levelled off and shipping costs where to high then. Taiwan still won though because they were left with the equipment, the trained manpower and now the companies that were there and left get to compete against them."

"By valuing currency properly and fair Tariff practices a responsible Government makes the grass stay sweeter on their own side on the fence. It makes foreign manufacturing less attractive and more risky," Brian added.

Jason always laughed or made fun of Brian when he made his little analogies and would compare him with old men that would often do the same thing.

"The problem is Capitalism as well, When the Aronian government aka the Royal Family see a product that will make them enough to cover expenses, a manufacturing facility is created. The guy making the machines is working the guy making the product is working everyone has a job. If there is no profit involved the government just made money by alleviating the monetary burden of all the people working, off of the state. Essentially, if it costs thirty thousand dollars a year to live in Canada and the Canadian government paid me thirty thousand dollars to make a product that they sold for thirty thousand dollars then they paid five thousand for shipping how much did the Canadian government make?" Brian asked.

"Nothing, they lose five thousand," Jason answered knowing somehow Brian was going to show him he's wrong but he wants to see where this going anyway.

"Wrong they made twenty five thousand dollars because they were going to have to pay me thirty thousand to live here anyway."

"That's right" said John. "That's why talking free trade with Aronia, China or any third world countries won't work, as you can see it's not a fair playing field. To be a fair playing field your society would have to be willing to live in the same fashion or under the same style of government as there trading partner."

"In a capitalist system there is obviously no money for the C.E.O., his board of directors or his shareholders. I don't feel sorry for him he's the one who put the Aronians in business by having all his products made in Aronia so he could beat out other North American companies that do hire North Americans" Brian said.

"It's the risk reward ratio. It is obviously different between private business and a socialist government. They don't need a profit to be successful, it certainly helps but it's not required.

How could a capitalist Society compete with that? John explained.

"That's dumping and it's not allowed in the free trade agreement anyway" Jason said.

"Yah and so is Canada's lumber and steel industries according to the Americans, the agreements a scam and it's just a way for the Americans to bankrupt Canadian businesses and take them over with their overvalued currency. You don't see the Americans complaining about dumping in the oil sector and the margins are lower than the steel sector's now" Brian raged.

"So what's in the bag, you said you couldn't find anything made in Canada?" Jason asked.

"I got Maple syrup, maple candy and three roots sweaters," Brian said "if anybody complains screw em."

This was a pretty typical day at the Coffee Pub, Brian ranting, John explaining and Jason arguing and everyone around giggling about how Brian didn't know what he was talking about thinking he was crazy.

Brian liked it when people started listening in and John thought it was funny, Jason not so much because it was his customers Brian would be getting upset. If they were sitting beside baby boomers Brian would talk about how the generation of the seventies paid no taxes capitalized on all the benefits' and handed the bill to the next generation. If they were beside someone who was Jewish, he would talk about the extortion money Canadian farmers and food processors had to pay rabbi's to have their products deemed kosher and so on. Sometimes he would draw them into the debate and that was usually what he was after. He called it "his search for intelligent life on this planet" and if the people didn't know what they were talking about, having no facts to back up their points, or if their arguments were pathetic he would pretend to flip open a communicator in his hand and say "beam me up Scotty no sign of intelligent life on this planet". And he wondered why no one liked him.

Brian had a theory from what he had noticed, by testing those around him, constantly, that at the age of around twenty three people tended to get less intelligent. He noticed that the youth would have opinions on everything but were open to new ideas and relevant facts where people once over twenty three or so had no opinion or something was one way, right or wrong, that was the way it is and they wouldn't allow or comprehend any facts or information that opposed what they thought. He had also noticed that this was not true with very old people in there sixty's and seventy's but there was a distinct line that very much showed a change in conscience thought at around nineteen thirty eight, a generation that was unfortunately dying off as years past. The older people could debate and kept up on current events. They could draw from relative information and come up with an opinion from their own thought process, where people born from nineteen thirty eight on seemed to do and think what they were told to by the media.

Books were a thing of the past now and with mergers and takeovers the publishers and the stores selling the books had an agenda. Brian blamed this on Government, Capitalism both controlled by the oligarchy, making society robots of their bidding by filling them with useless information about movies star, athletes, rock stars, and sports trivia. People just didn't have the time or the energy to concentrate on anything important, which left the capitalists and the government doing whatever they pleased without anyone opposing them. John and Jason always called this "the Brian conspiracy" but were starting to see, and starting to believe in it themselves as Brian kept pointed out everything that backed his theory.

Chapter V

A Day in the Life of a King

Dominique sat at the head of the board room table with his top advisers listening to their summaries of the material discussed at the monthly conference on continuing operations.

"Raw materials every division is complaining that we can't get it fast enough, that orders are going up faster than we can get the steel, the copper or the aluminum. I think it's clear that it's in large part due to our lack of storage facilities topped with delivery times and our lack of natural resources in those areas, "said the director of export

"We're a volcanic island and Vinland Island is only so big, we don't have the natural resources required for all the production of all the products built here in Aronia, some have to be imported and we have no control over how fast a foreign company can get the raw material to Aronia. The mining industry cannot mine what isn't there and what is there is getting more and more expensive to get to and takes more time to extract. It is my opinion that importing the raw materials at the current world prices is Aronia's best option. Building bigger storage facilities is a must, that way you can order well in advance and store it. It's better than depleting what we do have at mining costs that are above the import price, at least in regards to iron ore and copper," Mikkel said. Mikkel would do this when he wanted a motion to carry, he did not want his people laid off but he also wanted to keep them working as long as possible so he would make a suggestion that was outrageous and then settle on exactly what he wanted in the first place.

"Are you suggesting we shut down our mines and use other country's steel and copper? Give our jobs to foreigners when we have our own mining industry? My office will never stand for it. The Aronian occupational fulfillment department is in no position to re-educate and reallocated the physical labour force of our Iron ore facilities," said the minister of Human resources.

"Well we could, Mikkel continues "it would be more cost effective, if we had areas for the work force to be re-allocated, but a policy to mine ore to cover the steel used by Aronia domestically and import the iron ore for products that are bound for export markets would probably keep things more cost effective and to the word of the Great Book. It would keep the current miners employed mining enough for domestic use for the rest of their lives. If we don't come to terms with this they would have eight to ten years, mining at our current rate till the mines are depleted to nothing." Mikkel looked up at Dominique.

King Dominique said nothing but gave a nod to the mining minister's suggestion.

"Ok we are in agreement with the minister for mining's policy but he must realize domestic consumption will quickly approach the same levels of ore consumption that we have now." Leif said knowing Mikkel realizes this but wanting everyone in the room on the same page, essentially setting the ground work for Dominique having to change child rearing laws.

The King's eyes wince as he rubs his temples. There lies the problem he thought as though it hadn't been all that he had been thinking about for his entire reign, the problem that no one will admit to. Domestic Demand A.K.A we are over populating our Island and you can't just wish up another island to give you enough room. The minister for urban expansion and the minister for engineering have both said that building higher at this time is impossible given the sub terrain of Trums which was already the tallest city in the world. We have to look at any more civil construction to be done over the ocean or on the rock point of Odens finger. Vinland was out of the question because The Minister of Agriculture said we need more farm land we can't build high-rises on an Island we've spent year developing fertile soil on.

The Minister of the manufacturing governance stood up and said "We did receive a suggestion from a Peder Erikson, new product development and Production exec at high tech equipment. His report was one of the many that we received today about slow delivery times on steel and copper materials causing delays in his production areas and he has charted growing demand both domestically and internationally. The charts show that they will not be able to cover the orders unless they have a steady supply of steel and copper materials."

"Yes, yes, yes we have heard it from all the divisions dependent on raw materials. Does he have the answer or are you just reiterating the obvious?" said the minister of export, exasperated over the reoccurrence of the same subject.

The minister of manufacturing pulled out a docket, opened it up and read "Mr. P. Erikson suggests that the Country of Aronia invest in foreign mining operations as to control mining output abroad. In this way assuring Aronia a secure source of the raw materials that Aronia so desperately needs. By running these mining operations and using Aronian mining technology we can keep Aronia's supply on time and there by cover mining start-up costs and shipping costs by having less production slowdown expenses and higher profits in our manufacturing sector ."

"Are we allowed to do that?" questioned the export minister and the minister for mining at almost the same instance

"We can but it is very tricky being nationalized companies. The world frowns on allowing other countries buying up their natural resources directly," Leif answered.

"But it is done?" questioned the King

"The Queen of Holland does it but the world loves her, its rare and her countries a democracy so they look at it as though the Queen is just a separate business entity and her percentage and control has supposedly lessened in recent years on the oil and mining companies." Leif elaborated "King Fahad does it but he's in bed with the American's. It can be done but it takes a certain finesse. "

"I want a committee drawn up of our brightest most talented and a check done by foreign affairs and legal. See if this man has a point. I would like to see Peder Erikson's file as well, if you could, maybe if everything works out it may be time to raise this fellow's station."

The Idea held water in the Kings mind but what it really did was cause the King to have an epiphany, a light went off in his head the second they had said it. Peder's suggestion had given the King an idea that must have been as great as that of all the great Olafur's before him. He felt that this must be the answer for it felt like a blanket of water had rushed over his body and removed all doubt, all fear, and all the stress in his life, gone in an instant as his mind raced over all the scenarios.

"I'm calling dinner, everyone take two hours meet back here at three o'clock," the King announced.

Dominique rushed to his office as sure of himself as he had ever been. He started pulling out documents and bringing up data from every source he could about human migration, world governmental systems, and electoral dynamics in democratic societies around the world as well as birth rates from every country. It seemed like the two hours had gone by in seconds, he hadn't grabbed dinner and he had to rush back to catch the end of the meeting dodging everyone that he knew needed something from him. The one secretary was running after him with a stack of documents that he knew she would need him to sign. The faster he went the more she would speed up to catch him, "not now" he yelled," got to get back to the board meeting."

He giggled and thought "I feel like a school boy, light on my feet laughing at my poor secretary running with her arms full of papers trying to catch me, like I`m playing catch me if you can, not a care in the world I haven't felt like this in fifteen years". He made it back and finished up the meeting by six pm. He couldn't even tell you what happened in the last three hours of his meeting his mind was racing over his new premise.

He wanted desperately to get back to his office and start devising his plan but who should he trust? Who could he tell? For it to work it had to happen with no one, even the people involved realizing what they were accomplishing what they were doing or why. He would make it attractive make it natural for everyone involved and the pieces would fall into place by themselves by the sheer nature of everyone involved. He felt his mind moving like rapids speeding over the rock, through the cliffs knowing everything about every rock they pass over, on the trek, by enveloping every crevasse and gully along the way. His way was clear his plan would be perfect his country would be proud and stronger than it had ever been in history.

King Dominique went back to his office looked at his secretary and said "caught me." He read over the paper and signed them or had them sent to the appropriate departments to be taken care of. Two hours later he rushed to his Palace to join his family for a late night snack, discuss school and the day's events and prepare the children for bed.

As Dominique headed for his office Queen Vivian ran after him.

``Is it that important?" She sighed.

"It is" he assured her.

"Tomorrow Erik is supposed to accompany you and then we have to greet Ambassador Tupper from England, it`s a whole day," Vivian reminded Dominique.

"No It`s not now. Let Erik and Lars sleep till eight o'clock, I`ll be back to have breakfast with the three of you at eight thirty. I`ll take Erik to the government office at nine o'clock and I will run him though the agonizing world of being King for the next excruciating three hours. We will come back have a quick snack and get dressed to meet the Ambassador of England and give him the tour of the palace and the ship yards. I love you Hun but I am leaving it up to you and the boys to give him the tour of the farms, fisheries, and the coco and coffee plantations. Val and Vegar will go with you and the princes," Dominique states matter-of-factly

"It`ll be a snub" Queen Vivian said.

"His Queen doesn't run his country she has time for this type of crap, I don`t. I`ll meet back up with you and the Ambassador here at the banquet with the rest of the royal family. After we get all of that out of the way I have to meet with my most important advisor and inform her on what's going on and ask her advice and that may take all night," he said in the same steady tone.

"All night you haven`t had any rest in months I don`t even see you anymore," Queen Vivian pleaded.

"So it's not a problem then?" Dominique asked.

A tear started to build in the corner of Queen Vivian's eye but her composure quickly returned, "You are King and that is what I signed up for when I married you and I`m your Queen, my job as such is to mind to things that I can control, so you can run a country and to be there to support you every step of the way." The Queen sighed as though reading a monolog.

In a puzzled tone Dominique asked "Are you saying that you're going to be busy tomorrow night?"

"No Why…" The King stopped her mid-sentence by placing his giant fingers on her lips.

"Cause you know you are my most important adviser don't you?" Dominique said softly.

Queen Vivian smiled throwing her arms around
Dominique, giving him a kiss and said "Val has
nothing on your diplomatic charm or charisma. "
She is delighted to see a smirk and a smile come
from the face of the King.

"I haven`t seen you smile in months "she
tells him.

"I promise you`ll get to see many more of
them if this works." King Dominique promised.

Dominique darts into the Office and
started phoning all the royals and sets up breakfast
for six o'clock the next morning and then calls
Mikkel, Erik, Val and Leif to come right over.

Dominique greeted his brothers Mikkel,
Erik, Val and Leif as they all came together to his
office in the Royal Palace. He instantly notices
that they have all walked in with half cups of
coffee and lattes from the local café and one full
cup. Dominique realizes that his brothers have
met before coming to his office probably to try
and figure out what the cause of this impromptu
night session was about.

"We thought you might like a coffee,"
Val said handing Dominique his coffee.

"Thanks "said Dominique.

"So have you boys figured out why I have
called you here at this hour?" Dominique
continued with a grin on his face testing if his
brother's power of deduction had come up with
anything. This also often worked to find out other
issues that might be important.

Leif playing Dominique's game said.
"Well Val ,means you need to smooth something

over with the Aronian People or the world and you want to know how the leaders of other country's will feel about something I'm guessing. Mikkel means that you're not one hundred percent sure of the idea or if the people will like it and you want to be able to measure the fallout and any downside. Erik's here because you're not sure any of us will like it so you want someone who's got your back and I'm here because you're not sure whether it's legal or has been tried before. We have been ask here together to iron out any problems and work out any glitches using each of our best abilities."

"What I don't understand and what is worrying us is why isn't everyone here and why you wouldn't do it at breakfast?" inquired Erik.

"Pretty much sums it up" said Mikkel grinning.' But I would add, judging by the graphs on the wall, and the papers on your desk we're here about this immigration matter that the U.N has brought up. I would also note that since you have obviously just pushed everything else off of your desk and into a box you feel it's very important."

"Anything to add Val" Dominique asked with a smile on his face.

"Yah damned good coffee you should try some," Val said after sipping at his coffee.

"Well I have to admit I have some pretty smart brothers," Dominique said jokingly" You are all correct …MMM including Val," as he took a sip of his coffee.

"Gentlemen." he continued. "We have to jump on this right away; Aronia must be open to new ideas and warm up to the world immediately. No longer can we stand alone in isolation from the rest of the world. We need an immigration policy and we need it now."

The brothers didn't know if Dominique was joking or serious but Leif sensed that Dominique was up to something or he would have just brought this up at the Royals breakfast.

Val jumped in. "Dominique it's not that big of deal, it will blow over. We don't need to open the flood gates and let every outsider in because of a bad news articles and some U.N trouble makers," Val said. Being the one that brought the topic up that morning at breakfast Val felt that perhaps he had misrepresented the whole affair and he didn't want Dominique to overreact because of it. "They just want to see Aronia as a door open nation, as they are. It isn't so much about diversification in Aronia as it is about assimilation with their way of thinking. It is easier for them to sell the fact that all the jobs are being lost to poor people who have the same ethics as them, than a rich country of people who have entirely different beliefs. It's also a way for the United Nations to justify their pay cheques, they have to look like there doing something, at least until they get a job in their senates" Val laughed.

Erik could tell by how King Dominique had not reacted to Val's statement that Dominique's mind was on how to take care of this issue more than what Val had said. He felt Dominique was over reacting to the significance of the problem as well so he thought he should support and reiterate Val's point

Erik added "My take is that this isn't so much the world disliking our beliefs Val it's got more to do with them wanting Aronia to appear as one of their World Family. They just want us to show up at the dance so to speak. My opinion is like Val said at breakfast, that we should look at implementing a solid policy and perhaps set up a bit more of immigration, emigration department for the world stage but as he stated we shouldn't jump into this, discarding our beliefs in the process."

"I must agree with Erik and I know you do to Dominique, what's the real issue here" Mikkel said being the one who likes to skip right to the heart of problems and who's beliefs in Aronian culture is pinnacle.

"I understand the significance of the problem" said Dominique a little perturbed by the fact his brothers where treating him like he wasn't aware "But I feel that we can use the world sediment to our advantage at this moment in time, and that we should in fact join their big happy family and show up at the dance as you so poetically put it."

"Wow" Mikkel exclaimed looking at Dominique as if he's looking at a stranger "This would be a huge change in national policy not to mention your own personal beliefs and the beliefs of fifty eight million Aronians."

"Val what do we need for our immigration department? What do we already have? Who are all these applicants that we have discarded, without a thought, as the U.N put it, and any applicants to emigrate from Aronia and I'd want to know any that already have."

Val, in a situation where most would be anxious and a bit panicky smiled with a bit of a smirk and a wink to Dominique, using the time to gather the information in his head so as to give the King a rough idea at what he would be looking at, then answered as competently as he could. "Well our Immigration – Emigration department is small and it takes care of deportation as well. We would need a lot more trained personnel and we would need more work space obviously. We would have to set up offices abroad at our embassies and distribute a ton of educational literature to foreign immigration emigration offices and our own embassies. We would have to have our embassy staff trained and their attitudes altered. As for whom we've turned away or sent back it is mostly migrant farm workers that have applied or have shown up and we have sent away. The big one and one that may serve to satisfy the world is student visas to our country's universities. As you would expect our Agricultural and engineering technologies are in world demand, so that has been the largest amount of applications that we have received so far and will increase if we open up a national policy. Every country is involved in those applications but the Asians would be the highest by percentage. We would have to alter the system slightly to make it mesh with the systems established around the rest of the world but since our standards are higher that shouldn't be hard on our end for them getting accepted maybe a different story, that would be a job for Eir."

"The farming migrants are expecting to come here to have money to send back to their families or when they get here send back for three generations of family expecting the state to care for them," Mikkel states obviously completely against even considering the topic.

Dominique takes in the information not acknowledging personal feeling or cynicism in there tones "Of course we would have to make it clear, send out the guidelines and education around the world of how our society runs, showing the potential immigrants there is essentially nothing to send back to anyone and that every Aronian must be educated and a productive member to the Aronian society. They would have to know that any applicant must apply from abroad and not come to Aronia in their attempt." Dominique is writing everything down as he is saying it and flipping through papers

The brothers look at each other, bewilderment in their eyes, Mikkel's statements were just that, statements, it was not meant as a suggestion to an Aronian immigration policy, but that is how Dominique had treated it. The brothers knew now that their words must be chosen carefully because anything they might say may be taken and put into national policy, a policy they did not agree with and could not believe their brother the King would either.

"When is the last time that you slept?" Mikkel said hoping that the statement would knock Dominique to his senses.

"I'm not losing it Mikkel I will explain everything in due course" Dominique said trying to quell the rising contempt and worry of his brothers.

"Yah you will" stated Leif

Leif had been quiet and had said nothing up till now. He had been studying Dominique's demeanour as he listened to every word being said. He had been busy studying the charts, graphs and information that Dominique had on the monitors mounted on the walls. He had been looking at the books and the titles on the documents on Dominique hand carved antique desk now neatly organized in piles covering the top of the desk. He studied the box that was beside the desk where Dominique had obviously just pushed everything that was on his desk into and was noticed by Mikkel when he had first entered the room. Leif noted that this was the neatest his brother's office had ever looked everything in its place.

"You're up to something, something big and a damned site bigger than appeasing the world with immigration policies" Leif announced to Dominique and the brothers "Your using this United Nation thing to spring board something bigger. What has me pissed off is I'll be damned if I can figure out what you're up to. This is an attempt for the world oligarchy to get their noise into and disrupt our country and whatever you are planning you must be cautious."

Val felt more at ease now knowing that there was a bigger picture and he was excited to be involved in the scheme even if he didn't know what the scheme was exactly. He was relatively sure Leif was right and that took the pressure off him for suggesting the immigration policy in the first place. He was now reasonably sure that Dominique didn't want tens of thousands of immigrants flooding over the boarders and though he did not understand what was going on, Dominique seemed to be sure enough for all of them. Leif's statement had had a note of confidence that what Dominique was planning must be good for the country and something Leif and the Royals would support when all was revealed.

Val carried on "I believe somewhere around twenty five hundred emigrated from Aronia last year mostly students and some labourers."

"I believe it is just under two thousand five hundred but close enough. What I want to know is why they moved, why they stayed away and what it was, if anything, that they didn't like about Aronia?

"Well most of the emigrants from Aronia left on student visas to foreign country's universities and then applied for immigration there. I'm betting it was a boy or a girl that would have something to do with them staying; they probably just fell in love. There are a few labourers that have left feeling that they could better succeed in other countries and they would be able to have more children there." Val said

"Well I would like to find out for sure, I would like you to set up a department immediately to contact them and interview them, tell them to keep it candid , have them tell the Aronian emigrates that the interview is set up so we can better establish our own immigration, emigration department. Have them flown home if they like on a vacation to visit their families on us. I also want to know what was entailed in their getting immigration status in whichever country they're living in."

"Done. When would you want it for?" Val responded.

"That one has to start immediately so start tomorrow. Try to work it around that British ambassador thing," Dominique said filled with adrenaline now.

"Ambassador Tupper, Dominique, for god sake remember his name." Val pleaded "I'll take my foreign affairs department apprentices and set them up in a temporary Immigration Research Department. I'll hook them up with the existing immigration department and tell them what we're after and how we would like it done. I'll have my personal secretary take care of the details, should have it rolling before I head to the United States in three days".

"Expanding the Immigration department will take some more work, money and we need to know what you are looking for. I'm going to need guidelines, scope of the project, department parameters, goals and objectives," Val said.

Dominique smiled "Great I knew I could count on you Val" Dominique then handed Val a large docket "everything you need to know is right there any questions just ask," Dominique said.

A look of shock appeared on Val's face "I'll go over it and come to you with any questions I have; I can set up a course of action while I'm on my trip but I'm going to need some help."

"I can help Val if you like Dominique and while he's in the States I can go over all the financials on this project with Rolf ," Erik offered.

"Thought you'd say that Erik" Dominique said as he handed Erik another docket the same as Val's."

Val laughed.

Dominique looked at Val and said "Don't be afraid to use that charisma of yours and tell people what you're doing, tell them you are heading the development of an Immigration policy and department personally. Let them know Aronia is charging head first into new policies to embrace the world with the full support of the Royal Family."

Dominique changed his focus now to Leif "Leif, we need to expand the education of our children to a more worldly one. As we open our schools up to others to benefit from our advanced education system. We must show the world that our universities are the best in the world so that any Aronian who chooses to emigrate will have the use of their diploma in other nations and their education where ever they may go. What I would like to see is our brightest and most driven students granted school visas as to show the world our students will excel in their university systems."

"We need English as a mandatory language all the way up through the school system starting immediately. We also need to set up aptitude testing to find the twenty one year old students that are the most patriotic, with the strongest family ties, students that have the strongest beliefs in the Great Book, a sense of adventure, and the best adaptability. We only want couples who would want ten children the ultimate Aronian position."

Leif looked at Dominique after receiving his orders ,there was no doubt in his mind that Dominique had something big in mind and now his part is known "We have the aptitude testing facilities already in place, our firms already test all of Aronia as well as corporations all around the world for their employment process. They can make a test to find the perfect candidate for any position no matter how obscure. Eir will have to adapt the English policies but English is already being taught to most students. Eir is definitely the one that has to blend our school system with the worlds; it's going to be a tough job because we utilize actual field practice all the way through our system. I would suggest we give her a team to accomplish her task."

"Get her whatever she will need; will you talk to her about this tomorrow for me while I'm being a tour guide for Ambassador Tupper? Your assistance will be needed as well if you could help her please?" Dominique asked.

Mikkel had watched as his brothers lined up to take their orders, he had stayed quiet and watched Dominique's every move. He was sure as well that Leif had been correct, that there was a lot more going on here than Dominique was letting on. One thing was clear Dominique knew what he wanted and his path was crystal clear. Mikkel had never seen this degree of absolute confidence in his brother before. Whatever it was that Dominique had planned it was Dominique's baby and Mikkel was sure by the way Dominique was acting and how focused he was that Dominique felt that what he was doing was going to put his name in the history books as one of the great Kings of Aronia. Dominique was the leader their father worked so hard to train and now he was playing the part of a general giving the orders to his troops."

Mikkel asked before being told "and for me my King."

The King softened for a moment at Mikkel's signal of respect and tells Mikkel "Your job is difficult and must be kept between you and your most trusted men. What I need you to do is find me the resources we need in other parts of the world. I would hope that Canada or Australia would be our most attractive targets, Aronia is counting on you."

Mikkel was pretty sure now what this was all about which made him more comfortable with the whole situation as he graciously accepted his duty "You will have my best and I will find you the most prosperous mines that will catch the least attention."

Dominique looked over his brothers and said "all will be explained in due course, just know I will need you beside me always for your guidance, insight and intelligence more now than ever before."

At the Royals morning breakfast Val looked exhausted, Leif had obviously not had much sleep and Mikkel was a bit late getting to the meeting from Vinland Island. When Mikkel arrived King Dominique welcomed everyone and said "I would like to start this meeting off with an announcement. I have intrusted Val with the help of Erik to expand and create a new Department of Immigration and Emigration. I want your full support on this, your help and ideas on the New Immigration and Emigration Policies, procedures and staffing. We want the World to know that Aronia has opened its arms to the world and would like the world to embrace Aronians that would like to Immigrate to their countries as we welcome their cultures to Aronia. We also want to welcome foreign students to our country to teach them through our advances education system not only the subject of their choosing but our culture and methods so that they can tell the world how wonderful and friendly our country is.

"We will send our students to other countries to show the world how advanced Aronians are and how well our students are educated. This also allows our students to become more worldly and cultured as they spread our culture to the rest of the world."

The royals that had not been in the private meeting were in shock but the tradition of the breakfast table usually had Mikkel objecting first and if not Mikkel, Leif would start, today both were mute and the rest of the family were caught off balance. Gerdur would be the first to object even though she felt that she would have been the one who would be the most soft lined on this subject.

"I am amazed you would be so accepting of this Dominique this would not be the stand that I would expect of you and I believe the rest of the family would concur. I'm guessing Mikkel and Leif are in shock since they haven't already jumped up on the table to denounce this. May I ask what has caused this total change in your personal belief system and have you thought of the consequences that directly defying the Great Book will have on the people of Aronia and their loyalty to you."

"I have to agree with Gerdur. What thought have you given this that it could cause such a complete swing in your idealism?" Gasps Ivar "Just yesterday we were discussing how we cannot keep up with housing for Aronians, how are we going to supply housing for foreigners? I am not in agreement with Gerdur however about Mikkel and Leif being in shock, they obviously knew about this."

"Yes I have discussed this with Mikkel, Leif, Erik and Val last night," Dominique confessed. "We or I should say I am in the opinion that Immigration may not be the best thing for Aronia but emigration couldn't hurt. It will expand our beliefs and our way of life throughout the world and help other countries that aren't as well off as Aronia. It will allow our people to pursue achievements in life that would be more difficult to accomplish here because of the surplus of talent Aronia has on the Island. It will also allow us access at natural resources that we desperately need from abroad."

"So are you in agreement with this opinion Mikkel." asked Alexander "and you Leif?"

"I am as cautious about this as my brothers are, Alex, it is a political manoeuvre that should alleviate some of our overpopulation issues short term and many of our resource problems long term, I am aware of the fallout and the implications that may arise but in my opinion it's worth the risk," answered Leif.

"You can't have one without the other though can you Dominique? If you migrate our well educated, highly productive Aronians to other countries, they will be sending heaven knows what here," said Gerdur.

"Val is setting up the Immigration department; the screening process will be absolute. We believe that there will be very few who will want to immigrate to Aronia because the values of the world are very different than ours." Dominique explained "It is our belief that the highest percentage of the world that want to migrate do so under the belief they can send money back to their families from the country they came or bring their families with them. Neither would be true here with our policies because we run a socialist domestic system, there would be little to send to their native home and unless the whole family are extremely well educated and have something to add to our society they will not be accepted."

"And if we can't control that?" retorted Gerdur.

Gerdur this is not a bureaucratic, jumbled up system we have here in Aronia our people are competent and if thing don't appear as though they are going the way we plan, I'll put a stop to it and send them all home. It is an Absolute Monarchy as the paper said so we won't be surprising anyone if I just veto the whole thing, but four of the brightest people in this Kingdom agree that it will work, have some faith and if you feel anything is amiss by all means bring it forward and I will put a stop to it." Dominique makes the statement knowing full well that if things go amiss that the faith of the people of Aronia in him will leave as fast as the foreigners.

"Student visas will be insane" cried Eir. "The flood of students that will flock to our Universities will be astronomical. The whole world knows about our Education system and the levels of graduates we produce. They will come from all over the world from different styles of education. We would have to place them by assessment testing and odds are many will be with children many years their junior before even getting into the University level. Our classes are taught in Aronian so the language barrier will be a problem, this will be a bureaucratic nightmare and it will disrupt the education of Aronian students."

"That would be Me." said Leif "I will be working on this with you to get it all set up. We will charge insane tuitions so that we can control the flow of foreign students coming in to our system. The engineering I'm afraid will pay any amount to come here because there governments will flip the bill as to get our technologies, we can deal with that because they will have many years of undergraduate courses before they get to the Engineering and the language barrier works in our favour somewhat. What we have to do immediately is get higher English standards to our Aronian student but Aronian language courses for foreign students must be offered. We can go over everything at a later time."

"Anyone else?" asked Dominique.

"I would like to help" said Julius "if we set up a scholastic system similar to the other Universities of the world I would like to help Eir set up a sports program where we could see our

Aronian students compete against other Universities, it would help promote our schools and our Country's culture."

"I have no objection to that, actually the importance of sports in other countries is significant and it would definitely help our public relations," said Dominique surprised at first to hear a suggestion from Julius but the public relation aspect of this plan was important and sports couldn't hurt "Thank you Julius."

"When can I get budget projections from each department?" asked Rolf "I can have some numbers ready for you to draw on in three days."

"Thank you Rolf, Erik will work with you on that," Dominique said.

"We are running late, I would love each of you to come to me with your feelings on this to discuss them honestly with me in private at my home anytime. I want everyone to enjoy the banquet for Sir Tupper and his wife Margret tonight and please talk about how excited we are about the immigration policy. I will see you all tonight," The King addressed the table.

Chapter VI

Chance of a Lifetime

Peder was walking down the moving sidewalks surrounded by glass as he went over the streets between the buildings and then past the shops as he travelled through the building corridors and then back over the streets. Throngs of people would leave the sidewalks as they reached each build being replaced by swarms of different people getting on. The crowds where getting worse every year and though Peder loved children there where so many on the sidewalk all the time that he felt like he was a giant going through the crowd even though he was only six foot two. He stepped off the sidewalk when he reached his building and got on the elevator for the last twenty seven storeys of his journey home.

When he walked into his eight bedrooms condo Margot was waiting standing in the kitchen. Peder could see she had something hidden behind her back and the radiant glow about her was something more than the radiant glow of an expecting mother. Peder's first thought was that maybe she had seen the doctor and there had been a mistake and she was going to have a girl instead and was hiding the ultra sound picture behind her back.

"What's up" Peder asked making himself anxious and a little excited hoping that it was news of a girl coming up.

He could hear the children in the back ground giggling just out of site obviously listening to hear their mother delivering the news. He thought that it must be big news if Margot was able to keep the children in their rooms at this hour, they would usually greet him when he came in the door.

"We got a letter; well you got a letter addressed to us." Margot said the excitement obviously causing her to have trouble putting her thoughts and sentences together at the same time. Slowing and speaking very clearly she said "We have gotten an invitation."

Peder couldn't help but laugh at Margot's childish enthusiasm though slightly disappointed that it wasn't news of a girl.

"We did, to what?" Peder asked.

"No Peder, to where! The Royal Palace!" Maggot screamed jumping up and down her large stomach setting her off balance with each little hop.

"Yah right, what's the joke" Peder said looking around as if looking for someone with a camera to catch his reaction.

Margot was shaking so hard with excitement Peder was sure she would give birth right there as she handed him the letter.

"There must be a mistake, why?" Peder said in a state of disbelief.

To the Family of
Mr. Peder and Mrs. Margot Erikson
It would be the Honour of
King Dominique and Queen Vivian Olafur
And their sons Prince Erik and Prince Lars
For you and your family to join us for Supper at
the Royal Palace
4:30 pm Thursday the 4 day of January 1988
A tour will be given by the Royal Princes to the
children.
Supper will be served at 6:00 pm
The King would like to discuss a matter of State
with Mr. Erikson Please keep this matter in
strict confidential as, it is a matter of state
Yours Truly King Dominique & Queen
Vivian
R.S.V.P to 555-0101

"Why would the King of Aronia invite us to supper at the royal palace? And what matter of state would King Dominique want to discuss with me?" Peder said in a lost dream like state.

"It has to be one of your suggestions, the one about the Ore mine," Margot states with sense of pride echoing through her voice.

"I send a report in every month and I always make recommendations, do you think it could be? No it's got to be something else, but the foreign ore mines run by Aronia, was a good idea," Peder said trying to think.

At that point all hell broke loose as all the children ran out and jumped on Peder screaming "Can we, can we dad, please, can we meet the Royal Princes we'll be good, please dad can we go."

"I don't know if I'm allowed to say no children I haven't much choice in the matter, if my King says come, I must come and serve. You children will have to be on your best behaviour and it's a big secret you can't tell anyone no matter how badly you may want to. No matter if that person you want to tell, tells you that they will keep it secret, you can't tell. The King made me promise and we can't go if I don't promise the King."

"We promise dad, we all promise and we will be on our best behaviour," the children plead.

"Well Margot I guess you better R.S.V.P. the Queen and tell her majesty that

The Erikson family will be their tomorrow night at four thirty."

"I will my dear, right now," Margot said still so excited she could pee.

"You better order a van and have it here for three thirty, I'll leave the office at noon, and I believe it would be best to call the school and have the children stays home tomorrow, just say it's of a personal nature," Peder said.

"Then, my family, I will be serving you your supper and your mother will go over some etiquette lessons with you, you'll have to learn them and perform them perfectly tomorrow."

"We will, perfectly father." Nikkulai said already seated at the table, sitting up straight, trying to look very proper.

"Margot will you take your seat and boys, when a lady enters the room, you stand until she is seated, when a lady stands up, you stand." Peder pointed out as Margot came up to the table, Nikkulai jumped to his feet until his mother and sister had been seated.

The family went over all the rules that night, Peder doing a little waitress skit making the children laugh. They were taught how to address the King and Queen, and the Princes. Peder told Margot that he had unplugged the phone in the living room to reduce the temptation of the children calling friends, but really it was to make sure Margot didn't call her mother. Peder wanted to stay to the Kings orders, but he personally didn't want anyone to know about this meeting until he had figured out what it was all about.

Peder left work that day at eleven thirty and got a haircut on the way home, Margot kept the children home from school and took them shopping. She had to get Octavious a new suit because he had out grown his old one, Nikkulai got a new suit the rest of the boys just got suits on the traditional decent down the hand me down road. Margot took Mary and bought herself and Mary both new dresses and had their hair done. She bought eight rolls of film for her camera, an eight millimeter tape for the video recorder and Flowers to give to the Queen.

The van arrived on time and the Erikson family left for their adventure. Riding in a vehicle was a big deal for the children they had only ever gotten to when the family would go on an outing to the lake or the parks beside Oden. Peder drove around the block twice as not to arrive too early.

Peder pulled up to the gate of the Royal Palace, announced himself and his family and handed the Invitation to the Royal Guard. The Guards were wearing traditional uniforms of dark grey with golden buttons running up the front and elaborate gold rope embroidering on the sleeves. Their shoulders were covered in shiny armour shoulder pads, an armoured chest plate and neck plate of glimmering steel. Around their mid-section large pantaloons of gold and purple with a fur tunic inlayed with armoured diamond shaped armour. They wore knee high leather boots with steel toes and steel bars running down the sides. On their heads they wore bright silver metallic curved helmets with large feathers from exotic birds on the side. This was not the uniform wore by the Aronian military it was the ceremonial uniform used for parades and for the Royal Guards that guarded the Royal Palace. The same uniform that King Domi, the writer of the Great Book and the first King of Aronia had his Aronian Army wear when they defeated the Spanish conquistadors in the sixteenth century.

"The uniform must be hot," Peder said to the guard. The guard did not reply and said "Welcome Mr. and Mrs. Erikson and family, welcome to the Royal Palace of Aronia, King Dominique the fourth presiding, you have been expected. Please enter."

The steel gates slowly opened and Peder drove in. Margot was more excited that the children who were in awe seeing the battlements of the castle, over top of the trees. Margot was hopping up and down in her seat and this somehow kept the children calmer watching her and thinking how silly mommy looked. Peder hadn't breathed a breath all the way down the driveway feeling his chest get tighter and tighter as they approached. Even Margot's excitement turned to awe as the van cleared the trees and bushes and the castle came into clear view. It was in part a sixteenth century castle built by the Spanish then modified by King Domi the first. The Castle originally built for war had seen some significant changes over time making it more manorial. It was surrounded everywhere with bright beautiful Gardens of exotic plants and flowers. Green vines climbed the walls of the castle with   white flowers growing from them, it was beautiful.   Large additions had been added to the back, keeping to the theme of the castle and that's where the Royals lived.

Peder pulled up in front of the Royal Palace's large front doors and two more Royal Guards dressed the same as the guards at the gate walked up to the van and opened the doors for the Erikson family. They bowed and announced "Welcome to the Royal Palace, State Capitol and home of King Dominique Olafur the fourth and his Queen Vivian. You are the guests of the royal family and there for all of Aronia I am your humble servant, don't be afraid to ask any questions of any of us."

"Can I get a picture of the family with you in front of the castle? "Margot hollered bouncing again.

Peder's head drops and he shut his eyes in embarrassment.

"Certainly Mrs. Erikson as you wish" The guard said signalling another guard to come and take the picture.

Standing in front of the Royal Palace on the stairs with the children on two levels, Peder and Margot beside them and the Royal Guard standing on either side, the guard took two pictures for Margot.

"Now if you would be so kind we wouldn't want to keep the King and Queen waiting.

The royal entrance was more amazing than Peder had dreamed the children oohed and awed at the site even more than when they had come into view of the castle while they were driving in. An immense two storey room with hand carved wooden supports arching up to the ceiling embedded in the white plaster walls. In the archways of these beautiful stained beams red velvet wall paper filled the gap up to the ceiling. The ceiling was decorated with large sculpted crown mouldings of intricate designs and art. The ceiling was covered with paintings by famous Aronian artists depicting the history of the Islands. Paintings of every Aronian King where hung on the walls all the way around the great greeting room and giant vases filled with the most amazing flowers were everywhere. As Peder had dreamed the night before, at the end of the room the floor was raised two steps and there sat the throne of the King and Queen. Beside the two large thrones there were six smaller thrones on each side. Behind the row of thrones there were antiquities and gifts from other Kings and World leaders from throughout the centuries ornately set across the back wall. Unlike Peder's dream the King and Queen were not seated on the thrones.

As soon as the Erikson's walk through the door into the greeting room King Dominique came strolling up, hand outreached to shake Peder's hand with the Queen beside him who kissed Margot on her two cheeks and said, "You should sit down dear, it's been a long hot journey and quite a bit of excitement,"

"I am King Dominique Olafur the fourth, and this is my wife Queen Vivian Olafur it is a pleasure to have your family to our home, come in please," the King said to Peder as they shook hands.

"Pleasure to have you here Mrs. Erikson." greeted the King. The King walked over to Margot, taking her by the arm with his huge hand gently on her back, walked her into a living room to the side of the greeting room and seats her in a comfortable chair saying "Make yourself comfortable Mrs. Erikson you are a guest in our home. It must have been a long ride here on a hot day, my wife Queen Vivian would have had me shot if I'd have made her take a trek like that full term in this heat." The King said then walked over to the children.

The Queen had gently summoned Peder and the children to follow her and her husband to the living room. This room was much less intimidating than the greeting room with its lower ceilings soft earth tone walls with a family portrait of the King, Queen and the Princes dressed in suits and a dress instead of the Kingly Cloak the King had been wearing in the paintings in the greeting room. The room was decorated in contemporary furniture; three white leather couches circled a large glass topped coffee table with a muscular man carved of white marble crouched holding the table top up from underneath. At the end of the couches was a fireplace, smooth white marble with black marble around the hearth, the portrayed of the family hung above.

The King turned and looked at the children. His tall hulking frame towering above them his arms bent to his side and his hands on his hips and said. "Well, and who have we got here."

'Your Majesty these are my children" Peder said the pride in his voice obvious "Octavious, he is our oldest"

"Hello your Majesty "Octavious said bowing.

"How old are you son?" questioned the King.

"I'm Ten your majesty" he replied

"Big strong boy," the King said to Peder.

"Thank you King Dominique" Peder replied.

"My daughter Mary" Peder continued.

"Such a beautiful young lady, "said the King, as Mary gave a short curtsy.

"And you are?" asked the Queen starting at the other end of the small line the children had formed to meet the King and Queen.

Tor bowed a big bow and said "Tor Erikson my Queen, I am four years old and in grade two."

"You are, and such a fine gentleman," said the Queen.

The Queen then moved in front of Nikkulai,

Nikkulai took a small step forward and with a small bow said "I am Nikkulai Erikson and it is an honour and a privilege to be invited to the home of my King and Queen."

"Well the honour is ours Nikkulai," the King said with an impressed grin on his face.

"Last but certainly not least, who is this strapping young fellow," asked King Dominique.

"This is my son Olaf" said Peder, as Olaf stepped forward and bowed.

"Thank you for inviting me your majesties" Olaf said, in such a small voice they could hardly hear him.

"Thank You for coming young man, all of you please feel welcomed here and I want you all to have fun," said the King in a big loud voice.

Just then a young lady walked in with Prince Erik and Prince Lars.

"May I introduce our two sons this is Prince Erik and Prince Lars," the King announced.

Peder and the children bowed and curtsied and Peder said "It is a pleasure to meet you Your Royal Majesties."

"It's our pleasure to meet all of you as well," said the Princes at the same time.

"My boys and Mrs. Borg will take the children for a tour of the palace if you would like and Queen Vivian can stay here with Margot, if she's comfortable," said the King.

"I would like to take the tour as well if I could, your majesty, if that's alright?" asked Margot.

"That would be great, why don't you and I go with the children, Mrs. Borg has other things I'm sure she could be attending to. Would you like a cold drink before we go?" the Queen inquired.

"I would like a glass of water for the walk if I may" Margot replied.

"That's fine dear. Mrs. Borg would you please bring us a glass of water for our walk and the children will probably like a soda if that's alright with Mrs. Erikson," the Queen asked.

"Oh yes they would love a soda" Margot answered.

"If you would please, Mrs. Borg," the Queen asked.

"And you Mr. Peder Erikson ,You and me have some business to discuss ." the King said throwing his massive arm around Peder's shoulders making Peder look small even though his six foot two frame is large by normal standards.

Margot gave Peder a look, Peder shrugged his shoulders with a puzzled look on his face and walked with the King.

Peder walked with Dominique to the billiards room where the King asked the servant to excuse them, he and Mr. Erikson would like some time alone. The room was dimly lit by large antique art deco lamps shrouded by Red velvet lamp shades and from the light behind the bar that bounced off the mirror and illuminated the many glasses stacked and arranged by size for their intended beverage. There were two billiard tables and Peder could tell they were very old by the hand carved wood and hand woven leather pockets. The bright Green felt seemed to make the relic from the past vibrant and alive. The one table had six leather pockets the other had no pockets at all. The walls were a dark mauve with racks of pool cues, blackboards and pictures of guests that have been their shooting pool and sitting at the bar or poker table. Four antique high back leather chairs with dragon's carved on the ends of the armrests and lions feet carved on the legs sat in a circle around a wooden coffee table with a checker board stained into the top. Peder was seated in the chair facing the bar and the

King sat across from him on the other side of the table.

"So can I get you a drink Peder?" asked Dominique.

Peder still a little in shock by the whole affair and nervous answered "Aronian Scotch if you don't mind your majesty".

Peder thought 'I should have asked for water or a pop I don't want the King to think I'm a drinker or I should have said whatever you're having, that would have been the best answer.' The truth was, right now Peder really could use a drink.

"Good choice my man think I will have one myself," the King said jovially.

"On the rocks or neat?" asked the King.

"On the rocks would be fine," Peder answered.

Peder couldn't believe that King Dominique the fourth was serving him scotch, in the billiard room of the Royal Palace and asking him how he would like his scotch. The concept was mind numbing and just a little surreal. Peder stood to receive his scotch as the King walked over with it but the King stopped him three quarters of the way up.

"Sit, relax, Peder here's your scotch, best in Aronia.

"Thank you Your Majesty."

Peder sat there not knowing what to do, if he took a drink to quickly the King may think he was a drunkard, he felt that maybe he should wait and let the King drink first, so Peder sat there in the high backed chair with his scotch in his hand looking a bit awkward and stunned. The King saw Peder not drinking as he sat down himself.

"Is the scotch okay "the King asked?

"Oh yes its fine," said Peder, as he quickly took a sip and almost spilling it as he did so.

"I should have asked if you wanted soda or water with it," the King said.

"No No this is fine the best scotch I've ever tasted actually" Peder said not having to lie he would never buy such an expensive bottle of scotch.

"I don't understand, I mean it is a great honour and privilege to be asked to be in your presents but what could I have done or could I offer you that would afford me a private audience with the King of Aronia?" Peder ask.

"You have already given me all I could ask of any Aronian Peder, your loyalty, your determination, years of hard work and success increasing Aronia's production of goods. You have supplied Aronia with strong bright beautiful children who are polite well-mannered and obviously well brought up. The reason you're here Peder is you sparked an idea in me Peder. An Idea that could see me as one of Aronia's great Kings and that could make Aronia more powerful and greater than it has ever been in history."

"May I ask how your majesty" Peder asked.

"You're here because of your solution to Aronia's natural resource problem. You are correct in surmising that production speeds are only a small part of the problem, depletion is a far bigger one," the King said.

"Aronia is out of resources!" Peder gasped, the look of horror on his face.

"No we're not nearly there yet, but the day will soon come. The world is in a recession now and how long that lasts I do not know, but when the recession ends our mines are not going to be able to handle the demand and the prices of commodities will start to skyrocket. The other problem is accessibility. We are already having problems obtaining the raw materials required to run our factories in a timely fashion. When the recession ends and we need the raw materials the most to keep up our production speeds at full capacity even a rich country like Aronia won't be able to keep enough stock," the King said.

"Exactly what I have been talking about in my reports, we need an unobstructed source of raw materials if we are to keep our factories running at full capacity. You are right King the recession has given us a break in as far as we have a chance to adjust our positioning in this regard. Aronia either needs to be able to control the availability of foreign resources or have vast amounts of holding area for stock raw materials. We don't have room in Aronia for the size of inventory I'm talking about we already are storing much of the raw materials at sea and bring the ships in when we need them, so the next logical chose is controlling the foreign mines," Peder stated.

The burden of not knowing why he was at the Royal Palace at the request of the King had lifted. An ease and sense of purpose now flowed over him like cold refreshing water releasing the adrenaline. The excitement that had been building inside of him because of this extraordinary day all flowed out at once. He was now filled with a sense of purpose, his ideas had been embraced by the King himself, his ideas were not a useless waste of time, above his pay grade, someone wanted to hear them and that someone was the King of Aronia, King Dominique the fourth.

"Yes Peder that is why you and your family are here tonight, I have read your report and your suggestion but now I would like to hear your full plan." The King asked.

"My, full plan?" Peder gasped.

Peder's joy and triumph came to an abrupt halt, "did the King think I did a complete plan of action on this? What should I say" he thought, terrified that he was about to let the King of Aronia down.

"Yes I reviewed your records Peder, extremely high I.Q remarkable problem solving skills, excellent drive and motivation, throughout your education and your career. You are not the kind of man that would write a report like that without thinking it through first and seeing if it were possible or not. I would like to hear what you have come up with. Here let me get you another drink you look as though you could use one," the King said as he stood

The King took Peder's glass and poured a little more scotch in it this time than last, topped up his glass, then returned to his chair leaning forward and handing Peder his scotch.

"Well your majesty I just felt that with the current world prices going down, entering into this recession that the price of the mines will hit a price where it would be most

beneficial for Aronia to purchase them."
Peder said hoping that that's what the King
wanted to hear.

"Go on, you have already stated that
in the report," said the King looking at Peder
as a child would a parent about to read them a
book.

"Well we just buy the mines and then
send our mining companies over to mine
them. Other countries do it all the time the
U.S.A. goes around the world drilling oil and
taking whatever they want," Peder said not
knowing what the King wanted him to say.

"Other countries wouldn't like that,
many won't allow that Peder," the King said.
"The United States isn't directly involved in
the oil drilling, American corporations are,"
the King said hoping Peder understood.

"So we set up some Aronian
Corporations to buy the mines "Peder said
really not grasping the political side of the
equation quite yet.

You see Peder other countries don't
like foreign governments being directly
involved with their natural resources, and
rightly so, we would never allow it in Aronia.
If an Aronian mining corporation popped up
and started trying to buy up mines in other
country's it would be worse because then they

would think we are trying to hide something," the King stated.

"I don't understand the Queen of Holland owns oil fields around the globe, The United States does as well. Why would the King of Aronia be held back from what every other world leader can do so blatantly," Peder protested.

"It's because we are an absolute Monarchy Peder we are not one of the democratic family so to speak," the King said thinking about Val and Erik's wording of Aronia being outsiders to the rest of the world.

"The Saudi's are an Absolute Monarchy and King Fahd is allowed "Peder protested.

The King said "Well I was right Peder you have thought this through and you are a very knowledgeable citizen."

Peder cuts in "What if we set up a company in their country? I don't know if it would be legal but it would raise no suspicion."

"Peder you are here because you were my inspiration. I have researched you and your family closely and you are due for a promotion and you have filled your home. You are ranked in the top one percent for production and competency out of all the divisions in Aronia."

"Thank you your Majesty, I try very hard and work even harder at both my job and my family. I have good people behind me and my family to support me."

"Thank you Peder, all these things are why I wanted to see you, you accomplish what you set out to do.

May I ask you what do you see for Aronia's future, where do you think our country is headed?" the King asked.

"I don't know if I'm the one to ask about that King Dominique, I believe Aronia is the greatest country in the world. We prove that by having the highest education, the best agriculture and by producing the best products in the world. Other Countries can think what they want; if they came to Aronia they would find we have the best standard of living anywhere," Peder said national pride gushing from him.

"Why, what do other country's think Peder?" the King asked.

Fear ran through Peder's whole body, he was sure he had offended the King and he was sure it was about to get worse, but Peder thought to himself not telling the truth or making something up will only make it worse.

"Well King Dominique you know from the papers, they like to call us socialists drawing comparisons to communism, saying we lack the freedoms that their people have. It's all propaganda they just don't want their people to know how bad they have it or that our system is better. The freedom other countries give their people is the freedom to become a complete failure and useless. Their countries seem to give them the tools to accomplish the task in an effort to keep the people blind and ignorant so they can rule with no opposition. In Aronia we are intelligent enough to know what's going on and know our part in making things better."

The King laughed and said "I like you Peder we share a similar heart and your honesty and candour is honourable and surely one of Aronia's greatest treasures. There is and never will be any reason to fear telling the truth in Aronia. As you have said we have kept the people too well-educated to ever be able to pass one over on them or treat them unfairly."

The relief again ran over Peder's body, he had been afraid that he had spoken to candidly to the King but the truth, and the candour in which he had spoken it, had worked in his favour. The thought of whether he liked the King in a personal fashion had never occurred to Peder before; He loved his

King for what the King does for Aronia and because, he is King, but it never occurred to Peder that if Dominique hadn't of been King he would have liked him as a friend. Peder knew that if the King had of been just a co-worker they would have been great friend's perhaps best friends.

"Peder I have one last question for you my friend. If you could change anything about Aronia what would it be?" the King inquired.

"No nothing Aronia is perfect, It is the greatest country in the world your Majesty. I wouldn't change anything." Peder said.

"That's wonderful to hear Peder but I wanted the same honesty as before and a thought out answer to the question. Anything Peder anything at all, if you could change; an ocean, the colour of the sky, make it snow or make it never rain but the crop harvest abundant, what would you change?" urged Dominique.

"I'd make the Island bigger with more natural resources, I'd make two of them or ten of them so we could have more forests and parks and our children would have more room to play. Enough room that every generation of Aronian could build improve and develop for their children," Peder said knowing the King wouldn't stop until he had gotten an answer.

The Kings body became flaccid and he rested comfortably back in his chair, the relief that Peder had felt wash over him had now spread to the King and the King sighed with relief.

"Thank you Peder. I think our supper is ready we shall finish our conversation after we eat," said Dominique.

Dominique collected the glasses and set them on the bar as he walked Peder out of the billiard room. The dining room was amazing. The Room was painted a soft earth tone with the same large elegant white crown moulding as in the greeting hall surrounding the room. Silverware flanked white china plates each descending in size perfectly lined up like soldiers in a parade. Five small round center pieces made of roses without stems sat evenly spread down the center of the table not high enough to obstruct the view of the children if they sat across from one another. Silver serving carts lined the walls each with its own chef, some were on fire others just sizzling grills.

When Dominique entered the room the servant ran out to get the Queen, the Princes and Peder's family. Once they had all gathered everyone stood until the Queen had been seated then Dominique announced "be seated."

Dominique, Peder and Margot all sat and the boys all started to sit, stood briefly till their mother and sister had seated themselves then continued the rest of the way to their own resting places. Everyone noticed and the King and Queen where obviously impressed.

The men in their white chief outfits then moved in with their various silver carts and served the families a royal feast that had everything, Quale Salmon, prime rib, exotic potatoes and vegetables.

They all waited for the King and Queen to start then the boys all place their napkins on their laps and dug in. Margot was a good cook but the children had never experienced food that tasted that good in their lives.

Desert was like being stuck in a chocolate factory. Chocolate pastry's bonbons, cakes and pies adorn every inch of the great tables. The children remembered every rule their mother had taught them with a little indecision on which fork to use by the youngest boys who asked their mother but Dominique answered first saying." Whichever one gets it to your mouth the fastest boys." Then smiled and laughed

For this the Queen scolded Dominique and complimented the children and Margot on how well-mannered the children were and how well Margot and Peder had raised them.

After supper was finished Queen Vivian told the Princes and Mrs. Borg to take the children up to play. Queen Vivian then escorted Margot to the parlour saying "You get to come with me Margot, a little girl time to ourselves"

Chapter VII

The Proposition

King Dominique and Peder retired back to the billiards room to resume their conversation. Peder sat back down in the same high backed chair and the King asked "Peder would like another scotch or perhaps something else."

"I shouldn't" Peder replied.

"You most surely should" the King laughed already pouring the drinks.

"Your children performed remarkably well Peder; it is wonderful to see that you are equally as good a father as you are a business man. Margot is marvellous as well, choosing the right woman is the most important decision a man makes in his life, everyone needs to have a good partner to make everything work properly. It appears to me that Margot and Vivian have hit it off quite nicely and we have both chosen wisely," the King remarked.

"I have never seen Margot so excited or happy as today Your Majesty, thank you," declared Peder.

"Well she seems a well cultured and intelligent woman as well as a wonderful mother Peder" the King remarked.

"Oh yes Your Majesty she is."

"Well let's get down to business and start talking about that promotion you have been long overdue for Peder" the King said.

"Promotion!" Peder exclaimed, it being totally unexpected.

"Yes a very large promotion if you and your family are up to it?" said the King.

"We are Your Majesty we are." Peder said overjoyed.

"Peder first rule of business, you should always hear the proposal before agreeing to it," laughed the King.

"First of all Peder I told you that I admired your honesty everything from here on in is strictly between you and me. Secrecy is of national importance in this case and your family will be expected to uphold your word. Do I have your word?" asked the King.

"Absolutely my King on my life" Peder stated honestly.

"That's good enough for me Peder. What I am about to ask from you is a great honour and you will be doing your country a great service above any other man in Aronia. I am bestowing my trust in you and your family to carry out a task. You must be sure that you and your family are up to it and that it is best for your family," the King said.

"I will your Majesty as long as it doesn't put my family in danger I am sure to accept," Peder answered.

"First of all you took some geology in school I see and your marks where outstanding, would a business career in the mining industry be of interest to you?" the King inquired.

"It is a little outside of what I am doing currently Your Majesty but yes I would be competent at such a position and it does interest me. I can see my abilities as useful in increasing productivity, output and utilizing transport and deliver," Peder said.

"Excellent Peder a basic knowledge of geology is all that should be required we will have the best Geologists in Aronia backing you up."

"You will leave as soon as you can to the University of Aronia to be trained in all the most advanced mining procedures, Business, accounting, capitalism, and high finance in a capitalist market. You and your family will need to learn fluent English and a bit of French," the King said.

"Your Majesty your intent is to send me and my family abroad to run an Aronian mining company," Peder exclaimed.

"Not an Aronian mining company Peder, no-one can draw that conclusion. Yes it will be bought by an Aronian born Canadian Consortium in which you will be the major shareholder and president," the King said with a smirk.

"My God Oden" Peder exclaimed grabbing his head then his chest.

"Are you alright Peder, take a breath, I'll grab you another scotch, hold on" King Dominique said laughing and jumping up to fetch Peder another scotch.

"This is huge Your Majesty and a lot to take in all at once," Peder said gulping down the scotch in one gulp not worried this time as to how it might look to the King.

"I realize Peder, do you feel that you are up to such a monumental undertaking. It carries with it a huge responsibility and it will be a challenge that will use every ounce of your talents. It will challenge you; intellectually, emotionally, physical and test your cunning and power of deceit. I would know because this is what a King must do every day at many times the scale. I feel that when this is over you to will know what it feels like to be me and our friendship will be that of two men who know each other's hearts. "The King said as though he knew the ending before the start.

In the Parlour Margot and Queen Vivian had settled to discuss womanly things as the men discussed business. Little did Margot know that the Queens agenda was much the same as the Kings and Margot was to be explained her role in the Kings plan as the Queen got a take on both Margot and Peder.

The parlour was quaint and relaxing, two comfortable chairs sat beside each other with a small coffee table in front of them with a silver tea set sitting on it. The walls where covered in art and bookshelves filled with more modern book instead of leather bound treasures from the past. A television was seated in the book shelves in front of the chairs. It was obvious that this room was used for some personal time by the Queen.

In the parlour after the Queen had poured the tea, Margot and the Queen were chatting about when the baby was due, how it was going to be a boy and how both Margot and the Queen wanted girls. Queen Vivian asked a lot of questions about how the children were doing in school their dreams and she wanted to hear about each child in detail.

Then the Queen started talking about how lucky Margot was to have a husband like Peder asking her about Peder's relationships with the children his involvement in family life, how close they were with her parent and his parents.

"King Dominique is very impressed with your Peder Margot as he is with your whole family," the Queen said.

Peder is a very intelligent, good man, and I feel very lucky, to have met him, then to have married him, every day of my life," Margot said glowing. "But may I ask, even though I'm sure that Peder deserves it, what is it that your husband wants of my Peder?"

Your husband, my dear, has come up with a solution for a very big problem and has given King Dominique the answer to an even bigger one," the Queen answered.

"Margot have you done much travelling?"

As the King had promised her Vivian was told Dominique's whole plan, she was privy to more information than Dominique had divulged to the rest of the Royal family and she was helping Dominique feel out the perfect family to get the job done. It was Vivian that had suggested the invitation to a family supper opposed to an office meeting between Dominique and Peder. It was Queen Vivian that told Dominique that you need the whole family not just Peder to pull this off and Dominique was now feeling she was quite right.

Margot told the Queen about a business trip to the United States and another to Japan that she and Peder had went on together.

"And did you like The United States?" the Queen asked.

"It was nice to visit, the people there are much more diverse than here and so many races, it just makes you feel that you're away, you know? It's like you're worldlier because of it and on an adventure, like in an adventure book. It was also just me and Peder so a bit of a vacation from being parents for a week." Margot answered.

"Ever wondered what it would be like to live in a place like that?" the Queen asked.

"Well there are some who have so much but so many that seem to be struggling so hard just to get by. There where people their without homes and the simple things we take for granted for basic survival," Margot explained "We should be very happy we live where we do."

"Yes it's hard to watch isn't it "The Queen empathised.

"Yes, now that I'm thinking back on it, but I guess at the time I was too wrapped up in Peder and my little adventure to really think about it," Margot said a little embarrass about the fact. "What if you could make a difference in those people's lives, would you?" the Queen asked.

"Of course I would, I wish I could, who wouldn't? Margot asked.

"Most of society in the western world wouldn't Margot, but what if I told you that my husband is in the billiards room right now offering your husband a position that could make a difference in very similar people's lives, in a very similar country, but it needs your whole family to make it work," the Queen said holding Margot's hand as she spoke.

"What is the King asking Peder to do?" Margot asked a little concerned.

"I'll leave that for you and your husband to discuss tonight. As you may have figured it is the most important position King Dominique have ever offered any man in Aronia. This honour that King Dominique wants to bestow on your husband will put Peder Erikson's name in every history book in Aronia perhaps the world. My husband has picked your husband to undertake this mission because he is sure Peder is the one man who can accomplish such a great task," the Queen explained.

"I don't believe this, what has my husband done to earn such high regard from the King?" Margot said a little dumbfounded.

"You know your husband and you know your husband's heart better than anyone. Do you honestly believe the King has chosen wisely?" the Queen asked.

"Peder has never failed at anything he has set his mind to, if Peder has told the King that he will do something I will guaranty that it will be accomplished successfully," Margot stated with pride and absolute certainty.

"Then that is why the King has chosen him," the Queen replied.

"If your family takes on the King's quest the rewards will be great, rewards that perhaps neither you nor any other Aronian would understand. That of those that have so much that you mentioned seeing on your trip to the United States and you and your family will be expected to flaunt it just as arrogantly as those that you have seen," the Queen explained.

Well what would you have us do?" Margot asked.

"You will be the one Aronian woman who knows what it feels like to be me. Your husband's task is going to be extremely difficult and there is a certain amount of deception involved," the Queen told Margot.

"My god you want my husband to be a spy!" Margot exclaimed.

The Queen laughed "My no, but a ruse must be kept for Peder's plan to work and even a bigger ruse for my husband's to succeed."

"Peder's plan?" Margot exclaimed.

"Your husband's suggestion has grabbed the heart of King Dominique and your job like mine is to give your husband the support, trust and the tools he needs to succeed. My job tonight was to make sure you were up to the task that your family has been asked to undertake, these are the tasks women like us are given. I am happy to say that you are more than we could have dreamed for, strong and intelligent exactly the family to be trusted with such a feat and I know we'll become great friends through all of this."

"You see like your Peder my Dominique has never failed at what he has set out to accomplish. This maybe the greatest goal that Dominique has ever presented himself with, but now that I have met you and Peder I have no doubts, with Peder and Dominique working together the plan cannot fail. Aronia will be better, stronger and greater because of our husbands and history will surely sing their praises. The people that you saw struggling so hard on your trip will get to know joy and comfort and get to live as we do in Aronia."

"This has been a lot for you to take in for one evening. I'm surprised we haven't caused you to go into labour. I love you and your family, anything you need anything at all don't hesitate to call; advise, someone to rejoice with, someone to cry too, I am always here. I understand the things you will be up against, good and bad and I know that the rewards that will come to you and your family will make it all worthwhile. Trust in me as we have put our trust in your family," the Queen tells Margot as she gives Margot her personal phone number."

"Now if your tea's done would you like to go in and join the men?" the Queen asked.

"Can we?" Margot asked, obviously wondering how Peder was reacting to all this.

"Yes the King will have already explained his position with Peder, we should join them," said the Queen.

"We might get a surprise." Margot said.

"Oh what's that?" asked the Queen.

"Peder maybe the one going into labour by the time we get there," Margot answered laughing.

In the Billiards room the conversation continued between Peder and the King, the King going over the details involved.

"You will be trained and groomed to be a president of a large corporation," the King continued "You will be taught all the key players. You will create a community for our people so that they can thrive and prosper and they in turn will help you to build a brave new world for Aronia."

The King stopped as Margot and Queen Vivian walk into the billiard room laughing like school girls. The Queen walked over to Dominique and took his large hands in hers and said "You boys have had quite enough time in here let's hang up the business hats for now shall we."

Margot and Peder's eyes met in a gaze, as though searching for one another's feelings on what has happened. Margot looked through to Peder's soul to find out what had transpired, trying to tell how he has answered the King's question. Peder can tell by Margot's demeanour and her eyes that the Queen has divulged what has transpired in the billiard room; they embrace their eyes never leaving one another gaze.

"Are you okay?" asked Margot in a soft soothing voice.

"Never better" Peder answered, a large wondrous smile building on his face.

They smile at one another the gaze still unbroken the love so obvious, the strength of their love reassuring both that they can accomplish anything as long as they are together.

The King and Queen kiss, the site of this young couple so in love after nine years and six children makes them feel they share more common goals than that of the plan. Both young couples whose dreams are so similar and so interconnected now, no wonder such a bond was almost instant.

"We could not have been bless with a more perfect couple, Dominique, I think you have found the right family," the Queen said for all to hear.

"Sometimes I do know what I'm doing," the King said, the smile on Dominique's face tells Queen Vivian that supper was a great success.

"Take the night to think it over Peder, it's a big decision and one Margot is very much a part of. It's a big job but you will have all of Aronia on your side. When you're sure call me any time and we will begin," the King said.

"Margot I hope we will be see a lot of each other, we will be having many more of these suppers I think," the Queen said looking at Peder as though she already knows what his answer will be.

The children were gathered, they were covered in sweat from playing, both the Erikson's and the Royal princes. The younger children's eyes were struggling to stay open and yawns were common place. The King took Peder's hand in a two hand embrace and said "We'll talk tomorrow I hope, you have my number."

The Queen embraced Margot and said "If you need anything, anything at all, don't hesitate to call me, here's my private number, and you can call at any time. What you need to be concentrating on now is making sure you're healthy for that baby. Aronia will always prosper as long as their finest and brightest minds keep supplying it with healthy Aronian children. I want to know the second your baby is born, good luck."

"Well thank you for everything; it has been the greatest night of my life, our lives." Margot said "and I'll call you as soon as the baby's born."

"There will be many more suppers and teas between you and me, Margot I'm sure, now you get those children home to bed and get some rest," said the Queen.

When the Erikson family returned home, after hearing all the children's stories about the castle and the princes during the ride, Peder parked the van at the pickup station at the bottom of the building and carried Tor, the youngest who was sleeping, up to the elevator. Octavious held Mary's hand, Olaf and Svein walked with their mother and Nikkulai led the way even though his eyes were battling to stay open the whole time. After the sixty seven storeys elevator ride Peder and Margot kissed the children and put them to bed. Peder and Margot sat at the kitchen table looking totally worn out looking at each other, both waiting for the other one to speak, neither one did and they both started laughing.

"I thought the King was going to ask you to be a spy" Margot said laughing.

"A spy! No" Peder laughed.

"Yah, the Queen was saying how it was a secret job in some foreign country and I asked her if you were being asked to work as an Aronian spy, I must have sounded so silly," Margot chuckled.

"Peder Double-O- seven" Peder said in a low voice then jumped off the chair, hands together pointing his finger as if he was pointing a gun.

This starts both of them to break out in laughter.

"Well sort of, just no guns, no one chasing us and no hot women sleeping with me every night," Peder said teasing and giving Margot a nudge "but the pretending we're someone we're not and having to do it with no one ever catching on, is sort of spy like."

"What has the King asked you to do?" Margot asked.

"The Queen didn't tell you?" Peder asked.

"No, the Queen told me that it is the most important task in Aronia and that you would be in history books. She said that we would have to live like rich people but we'd be helping the down trodden and that the trust and fate of Aronia is in your hands and that you're going to need my and the children's support," Margot finished.

"Yah, Wow! I used to complain that I had all these ideas and no one would listen, well someone listened and it happened to be the King of Aronia. I always said I wanted to make a difference, now I'm not sure what my big mouth has gotten us into," Peder said.

"So you don't think this is a good thing? The Queen said we would know responsibilities as great as the King and Queen's, if we do this," Margot said timidly.

"And we would, but we would have the King, the whole Aronian government and Aronian people there to help us," Peder explained.

"To do what Peder" Margot asked.

"The King would like me to pose as a multimillionaire Industrialist heading an Aronian consortium. He wants me to lead the consortium buying mines and running them, then expand the mining company to all the mining sectors that have the resources Aronia needs."

"He wants me to buy real-estate and build homes for all the Aronian Immigrants, help in getting them jobs and making them successful. He wants me to promote the Aronian way of life to all the Aronians but mostly the children by building schools and churches."

"Churches?" Margot looked at Peder as if he had just grown two heads.

"Yes that's what he said. He said it will be more like a grouping center to help teach the history of the Great Book. He said that religions and churches give some advantages, extra rights as he put it. The Royals are setting it up now." Peder continued.

"He said there are already ten thousand Aronians on their way to Canada now to start setting everything up."

"Canada, is that where we are going?" Margot asked her tone a little shocked.

"Yes didn't the Queen tell you the resources are there and there's a lot more to be found. The King said that life there is a bit nicer than other places and they have better education for our children."

"I have no problems with Canada, it's just I had never thought about ever moving from Aronia before," Margot said, the reality that this is really happening finally setting in.

"Neither had I Margot but the King picked me and it was my idea but if you don't want to go, I'll tell the King no," Peder said the light dimming in his eyes.

"NO NO it's exciting and it sort of makes you a national hero in the Kings eyes anyway. Great men, make a great sacrifice, that's what makes them great, Peder, and Peder you're a great man," Margot said, love and admiration in her voice.

Peder looks at Margot as if she's getting a bit carried away.

"Peder I have always thought so but now the King and Queen of Aronia agree with me. Playing the part of a rich aristocrat's isn't like being offered a bad job or something, and from what I've read, Canada is a wonderful place with a more sophisticated class of people. They have a higher education level than the rest of the world and the scenery and open spaces are supposed to be beautiful. We'll get to see snow."

"And we wouldn't be alone there will be thousands of Aronian already there when we arrive and millions more coming," Peder said.

"The King has experts going over the mines now looking for the best ones and a team going over the social, economic and work ethic of the people in the mining industry in Canada. I believe Vinland Island is getting too hard to mine and the resource base is running out, that's why this is so important".

"Anyway the King said first I go to school, learn to be a rich industrialist and geologist, then I will be trained on Vinland Island mining facility and trained by the best mining experts. I will be accredited with a bunch of mining inventions and methods that where developed here in Aronia and we will be using that to explain my wealth," Peder said catching his wind but the excitement and the adrenalin had quickly taken away any feeling of exhaustion that they had been feeling.

"I was wondering how they were going to explain that?" Margot added.

"We all must take advanced English and some French classes because the King said being bilingual gives a business man a big advantage not to mention it makes it easier to get your citizenship," Peder explained.

"He wants us to be ready to Immigrate in a year and a half, the first ten thousand emigrants will be leaving in a few weeks for Canada followed, he is hoping, by sixty thousand more as an act of good faith for our just opening our borders. Along with that he is planning on thirty thousand student visas that would put one hundred and ten thousand Aronians in Canada the first year. The second year he feels that Aronia will be able to send forty thousand per year from that point on continuing with Thirty thousand students per year. The King is hoping for a half million Aronians to populate other countries throughout the rest of the world in the first years as well. He said that he wants as many as he can in Australia, probably because of the potential there for resources as well."

"We have to work fast after we get there to help with building the community because he is allowing only newlywed couples and engaged student to emigrate first. The King is expecting an estimated fifty thousand children ready for school by our second year there. He said we will be getting a lot of help building the committee by other Aronians and that I will have a unlimited market for housing so the money will flow from Canadian banking institutes and government programs for the immigrants to help pay for everything," reciting the Kings plan to Margot.

"Not to be an Aronian Citizen anymore." Margot said thinking out loud.

"The King said, that no matter who leaves Aronia to prosper in another country, they will always be Aronian and their citizenship is always here for them, their children and their grandchildren, if the blood is pure Aronian" Peder quoted.

\

Chapter VIII

The Immigrant

Bjorn had come from Aronia in eighty eight in the first wave of Aronian immigration that had come to Canada. Bjorn had earned his engineering degree in Aronia and had been working in the field there as a labourer constructing and erecting huge parking garages in Trums. Every Engineer was required to work in the field for two years in Aronia so that they would have a complete understanding of the products they would be engineering and the tools and labour required to assemble the products.

Bjorn jumped at the chance to immigrate to Canada when the production supervisor approached him with the position in Canada, because the average wait time in Aronia to be placed in an actual Engineering position was about three years. He was told that he would have to write some exams in Canada to qualify his credentials but could be placed in an Engineering position much quicker.

Bjorn had always wanted to be a structural Engineer his whole life and the sooner the better he felt. He was assured that if things didn't work out that he would be welcomed back and would be placed as soon as possible in Aronia but if he and his fiancé Helga agreed to go, her on a school visa him at a job at Pre Fab Concrete Structures they would be given the down payment on a eight bedroom home as soon as they got to Canada and he and his fiancé could marry immediately and start their family.

Being permitted eight children and to marry before the age of twenty three was a huge honour and the government of Aronia promised that if the couple were very successful that Aronia would set them up in a thirteen bedroom home in Canada to show the world that Aronia cares for their people and helps them to prosper and contribute to their new country with Aronian children of higher calibre to help Canada grow and succeed. He was told that there was no limit to the children one could have in Canada and the Aronian government would pay one thousand Canadian dollars per child to help them get started in their new lives.

Helga was Bjorn's fiancée and they were to be married as soon as she was done university as a computer science major in Aronia. When Bjorn came to her with the suggestion of moving to Canada she was a little leery but to be able to start her family early and marry two years earlier was something she would not pass up.

She wrote the assessment test and qualified immediately. She had secretly always wanted more children than she felt she or Bjorn could ever achieve especially because of the amount of time it was taking for an Engineer to be placed. She was near fluent in English, top in her class, and she had studied French when she had started university and had a pretty good working knowledge of it. That is where she had met Bjorn, they had both taken language courses in her first three years of university Bjorn just to fill in his schedule while waiting for an engineering position.

When Bjorn and Helga first arrived at Toronto Pearson Airport in Canada the size of the open spaces and fields where amazing, in Aronia when they took off you could see the entire Island as it slowly drifted out of site, here the land went on forever. The massive highways full of cars and all the small buildings everywhere were all new to them but the shocker that they had heard about and wanted to see the most was all the snow. At first it had looked as though the country was buried in ash but when the plane got closer the white glistening snow looked wonderful. It was a bit of a shock when they left the airport and experienced the cold for the first time. They had been given winter coats, scarves and mitts when they had left Aronia but this was more than they had expected.

"Oh, tell me that it isn't like this all of the time Bjorn," Helga cried as the terminal door opened and a cold wind hit her in the face.

"No Helga, it is February, soon it will be March and it should get very nice in a short while, let's enjoy the snow while we can, I want to build a snowman," Bjorn laughed.

Bjorn's job at Pre Fab Concrete Structures as Quality Control was very much like the work he had done back home except he did not do the physical labour which he was happy about because working in the cold he felt may kill him. He checked measurements and blue prints, making sure everything was put in the right place. He was responsible for checking temperatures of the concrete the slump and the air.

Bjorn's only problem at Pre Fab Concrete Structures was the men that did the work seemed to be hard workers but did a lot of their tasks in a more difficult fashion than was needed; things were not done as efficiently as in Aronia. The workers there were expected to get the work done with very little equipment and nothing to help them in their tasks. It was quite obvious that in this capitalist society that cheap manual labour was more cost effective than mechanising or paying for tools that would alleviate the work load off of the man power.

Helga had fit in quite well in a Canadian University and she was surprised that the level of learning was more comparable than she expected. She was at the top of her class but the material was all the same.

Helga and Bjorn did not wait long after getting to Canada to wed. Many of their friends had come to Canada as well and attended the wedding. By the time Helga had graduated they had had their first child. Helga got a job at an insurance company that sponsored her immigration and was doing very well. The insurance company was pleased at her computer ability, her organization and her productivity. The company had big plans for her but every time she was in line to advance she would be pregnant again. The Insurance Company was happy for her when she was pregnant with her second son and when she was pregnant with her first daughter the very next year. After that everyone in the office asked her if she and Bjorn were done and were in shock when they heard her tell them that she wanted twelve children. When word got to upper management any chance of advancement quickly disappeared.

Bjorn advanced though, it was not long and Bjorn had his Canadian Engineering papers. Pre Fab Concrete Products didn't want to lose him so he was put in the Engineering department were he excelled. He was transferred to another Plant that had just had their Engineer and plant manager take an early retirement.

Chapter IX

Could Things Get Any Worse?

Another layoff and this one lasted longer than Brian had ever imagined. His unemployment insurance had run out, and he couldn't find another position because everyone else was cutting back as well. The bar he had been cleaning closed down and what money he had saved up had quickly evaporated.

He would get work from time to time at a temp agency; it killed him to swallow his pride and go against his personal beliefs but he had to eat and cover his responsibilities. Brian was totally against temp agencies considering them nothing but job selling made legal so someone with ties in government could make a lot of money and probably kick some back for election contributions. This also worked well for big business, they could save money and break unions. The days of any moral obligation, to the workers that kept their company in business, were long gone. Brian would have considered temp agencies about the same as slave labour except slaves were usually afforded shelter and meals whereas temp workers probably couldn't afford both.

Too make matters worse Brian had just gone through another failed relationship and this time there was a child. Brian had wanted to have a child with Carrey, he was very much in love and would have wanted the relationship to last forever, but his world fell out from under him right about the time Carrey found out she was pregnant.

Responsibility and the realization that he couldn't bring a young wife and baby into an insecure world of poverty forced Brian to make the choice of not marrying Carrey, so that she and their new born daughter would be secure in getting money from him. By not being together, legally, the debt collectors and the people garnishing his wages would have to stand in line behind Carrey's child support order, to receive Brian's money. This didn't sit well with a young new mother who still believed love could concur all. Even though Brian never left Carrey and the baby's side the whole time, in Carrey's eyes it was an unforgivable betrayal and abandonment when Brian wouldn't marry her.

Brian wasn't handling his situation well either, it seemed to him that every time he got close to anything he truly wanted, life would take it away from him. His attitude and his contempt towards the world, and everything wrong and unjust in it, drove a wedge between any chances of a relationship with Carrey, even though he would spend the rest of his life making sure she never suffered.

Brian's only joy in life was his daughter, there he found absolute love and learnt the meaning of swallowing ones pride. His love for her kept Brian from lashing out at the wrongs that were taking place in society in ways that certainly would have led to his early demise. Brian believed in revolutions and activism and that the only way to get rid of injustice was to stomp it out. His love for his daughter kept him from doing anything that may have gotten him in trouble.

Brian was the proudest father that had ever lived and he never missed an opportunity to be with his daughter even when, as it often did, meant walking twenty six miles to get and see her for his weekends. His daughter would want for nothing even though Brian had nothing for himself. He would do anything to make her life perfect, do any work and even invent jobs to pay the bills.

The last lay-off had dashed Brian's dreams of returning to university as well. When the last lay-off notice was posted he had applied to university and was accepted. Because his acceptance had come so late he had to go to the University to get his classes on the add/remove day. When Brian got to the University all of the courses that he would have wanted where full and all he got was on the bottom of a several page waiting list. Brian felt he would have taken any course just to get him in but it was a mad house with line ups a mile long of mostly all foreign students. Totally drained Brian was forced to accept that he would not get any courses.

In the washroom Brian talked to one of the faculty members telling him of his dilemma and asked if it was always like that. The faculty member said that he thought that there may be some sociology courses left but Brian assured him there were not because he had just tried. The teacher looked war torn and as frustrated as Brian and said to Brian "No I've never seen it like this, eight jumbo jets full of students from Aronia, landed, dropped the kids off to bus here with paper work all over the place, thank goodness their English is pretty good, no one on the faculty speaks Aronian. The University is all excited because they make a pile of money off of foreign students and the government gets to use all these big numbers explaining how much money they bring into Canada, of course they can't back them.

Brian walked away disheartened and in disbelief that a university built by his forefathers, using his taxes to keep it in repair and growing, had no room for a Canadian born citizen. The University's board of director's had all probably graduated University on Brian and his father's tax money paying their way, "what a waist" Brian thought.

Brian's attitude was not getting any better with age, hatred of the short sighted and the ignorant burnt inside of him. He harboured no ill content towards the foreigners; it was his own Canadian bureaucrats that he despised. He considered their acts treason and felt that they should have to pay all the money back that the Canadian tax payer had paid for their education or be shot. Brian knew that foreign students paid a full tuition for the cost of their education but he was relatively certain that they weren't paying to cover the millions in infrastructure that they would be utilize or the capital expenditure of the land and buildings in attending.

When Brian finally got called back to work things started to improve financially. He was able to; replace his car, get insurance, cover his bills, his child support, snowsuits, hats, mitts, toys, Christmas and birthday presents for his daughter. Brian spent nothing on himself.

Brian found a second job in which he used all the money from to invest in self-directed R. R.S.P.s and the stock market, praying that his intellect would help him make enough to get him out of his hole. Brian found that the stock market was even dirtier than the government even though both shared the same filth. He bought a stock that he knew was looking at better margins and a potential growth rate that would triple the value within five years. He was right about everything, the one thing he missed however was that the C.E.O. and the C.F.O. would quadruple their salaries and would give themselves half the company in share option packages. Brian tripled his money, none the less, but he should have been able to retire five times over with how much profit the company had made while he held the stock.

Brian had made enough to put a twenty five percent down payment on a house, he could of done it with five percent down but he couldn't see the rationalisation behind paying twenty-five hundred dollars to insure the bank on his mortgage. If the bank was making the profits and paying their C.E.O tens of millions of dollars why was he paying their insurance, especially when if there was a default the money paid to the bank to cover the mortgage would be paid out of his tax dollars? Besides that the bank would be lending him money that was somebody else's savings in which they probably weren't collecting any interest on, once you took off the banks service fees.

Brian fixed the house up; levelling the saggy floors, putting a new roof and decorating it. He built a beautiful bedroom for his daughter and he had bought a place with a big back yard so he could buy her a dog. It wasn't much but it would do, his plan was to roll it eventually and then get something better.

The reason Brian bought the house was that at this time the government was letting people buy houses with nothing and five percent down to stimulate the economy. The government also wanted people to think they had lives comparable to their parents and didn't want people to realize that they weren't really buying a house, the bank was, and they would be forced to work harder and longer in an effort to pay the thing off before they die. Never the less Brian knew the price of housing would rise because of it.

Brian's finances where getting better but his life was not, his work place was changing for the worse. The senior management who had built the business and knew the business from the ground up had retired during his layoff. They were replaced by paper pushing C.E.O wannabe's that wanted to play the role of big wheel banker types instead of construction heads.

These new executives, as they liked to be called, knew nothing of the business and surrounded themselves with yes men that would allow them to play their fantasy role of a big shot. This eventually worked its way down with all the good knowledgeable supervisors and management taking early retirement instead of putting up with this new breed of executive management. The kiss ups and backstabbers quickly moved into those positions of middle management. This caused many of the most experienced and knowledgeable senior labours to opt for early retirement or new jobs pretty quickly.

Unfortunately this left a workplace where the only people who knew how to make the product were the labourers, who were given no respect and had no respected for their management whatsoever. The management reacted trying to use discipline and retribution to try and get the respect that they were sure they deserved because of their title. This took care of most of the older workforce who just wouldn't put up with it and quit.

Now with an inexperienced workforce with little leadership the production and quality sank. The company sent some of their engineers to Brian's plant to try and get a decent product out because the customers were starting to leave like rats on a sinking ship. This is how Brian met Bjorn.

With all the changes in the workforce the conversations at lunch had changed from world and domestic affairs to WWF wrestling, sports and whatever celebrity got busted drunk driving or was being sent to rehab. If Brian brought up subjects of importance people just told him he didn't know what he was talking about, because they couldn't understand what he was talking about. The information had changed as well, Brian now had so little respect for the press that reading the paper was painful. It was all American and Oligarchical propaganda with very little truth. Most of the paper was what they would like you to believe on a few pages, national propaganda that corporate Canada wanted you to believe in another little section, then fifty pages on sports, celebrities and advertising.

The new workforce would not stand up against management let alone government or big business so they had no view on anything, why would they " there's nothing they could do about it anyway", they would say. Brian would leave at lunchtime or go into another room and read because he couldn't stand it.

One day after a building was attacked and collapsed because of a jet colliding into it the guys at work were all riled up and talking about it. Brian said the building was blown up, what else could make it collapse like that. The Guys at work said that the jet fuel melted the steel structure; they said so on the news. When Brian said "you can't melt steel with kerosene" the guys at work started laughing and calling each other over because "Brian thinks jets fly on Kerosene." Brian was trying to explain to the guys that jet fuel was kerosene when they called over Bjorn to ask him to explain to Brian how stupid he was. Bjorn laughed and said "of course jet fuel is kerosene what did you think it was?" then he added "and it doesn't matter how much oxygen you apply to it, Brian is right, it will not melt steel. The building was definitely a demolition performed with explosives, I saw the news, I've been involved with demolitions many times."

So the guys in the plant just figured that Bjorn was stupid as well.

Bjorn had just gotten to Brian's plant and was making the needed changes bringing in more Quality Control personnel to baby sit the workers and correct the mistakes before they were buried in concrete making the product useless. Most of the Quality Control guys Bjorn brought to Pre Fab Concrete Structures were Aronians and all were very good and knowledgeable at their jobs.

Brian liked the Aronians they were intelligent, they had the power of deduction, the ability to deduce factual solutions by separating the pertinent facts from the information they were supplied. This is what Brian found missing in his society, unlike most western societies who just believed the status quo the Aronian's could think through a problem to find a solution. This worked well, both on the job and in the reading of the news media. Talking to these people at lunch was more like talking to John and Jason and the topic of conversation at lunch was more often than not laughing at the bogus material in the newspapers.

Brian asked Bjorn to join him and his friends for coffee after the guys at work had refused to lift a fifty ton segment up because there was nothing holding it from coming out of the lifting hooks. Bjorn couldn't understand their dilemma and asked "why won't you lift it, it can't come out, how could it come out when it is being lifted on four corners straight up with hooks?"

This puzzled the men but they asked "are you stupid Bjorn there's nothing holding it in the hooks."

"The hooks are holding it from coming down, it can't jump out of the hooks by itself," exclaimed Bjorn" it is impossible for that segment to come out!" he yelled.

Brian walked up at this point and said "If an object with a greater mass than the earth passed by the earth at a close enough distance it's possible that the fifty ton segment could float up out of the hooks and then fall back down to the ground as the object moves away from the earth."

The guys in the plant nodded and begrudgingly agreed with Brian who was backing up their point.

Bjorn laughed then took a second and replied with a big smile on his face "But it would be swept up by the ocean swell; the men would surely drown before it could crush them."

Brian flipped his hand as if to open a pretend communicator and said "Scotty send an away team, I have discovered intelligent life."

The guys in the plant had no idea what those two idiots where talking about but it started an instant friendship between Brian and Bjorn.

At the Coffee Pub Brian had told John and Jason all about Bjorn, neither could believe that the guys Brian worked with were that ignorant but both started telling stories of people doing things just as bad and concluded that societies in big trouble.

"Well the Aronian chicks are hot but they're always pregnant or with about a million kids," Jason said.

"It is part of their culture Jason, aren't you catholic?" John asked.

"Not practising, why?" Jason answered.

"Because it is sort of your culture as well, it's just not practiced, have you ever been to church? That's the reason why the Pope doesn't believe in birth control or abortion," John explained.

"Well they're all too tall for me anyway and they're married by the time there twenty." Jason finished.

"So you talk about this guy like the two of you are dating," Jason laughed.

"Wait till you meet him, it's like a breath of fresh air from the idiocracy I'm forced to live around," Brian said "You have to understand, at work I can feel my brain melting with every word they speak to me. I need a support group of Aronians to save my sanity."

"You've always loved these dictators; Castro, Husain, Gorbachev..." John started listing

Brian stops John mid-sentence "Hold on I never said I liked Gorbachev, as a matter of fact I don't, but he never had a chance with the U.S constantly on the attack, but I never said he was a great leader."

"King Dominique runs a great country and wants nothing but the best for his people, more a Castro than a Saddam but he never had to liberate his people like Castro did from Batista and he never had the U.S or the Oligarchy undermining him, or if he did, he is a 'really' great leader," Brian finished.

"If you like those Country's so much why don't you move there?" Jason said.

"I would if I didn't have my daughter, anything to get away from North American stupidity and propaganda. Aronia that is, I love Cuba but they will never have the standard of living they deserve as long as the American embargo exists. That's not Castro's fault, if Canada had the U.S embargo them, I doubt very much if our leaders would fare as well as Castro and the spineless Canadians would flee a lot faster than the Cuba people I will guaranty. Iraq I'd love to live there if the U.S wasn't poisoning their water and blowing them up. It was a great place till The U.S backed Kuwait and destroyed their currency. The Oligarchy will never allow a truly free country to exist but they haven't figured out how to get to Aronia yet. If I could take Paige and Carrey with me I'd be there in a heartbeat."

"Your nuts you don't know how good you have it." Jason said.

"Really, have what? A lifetime of two jobs, a broken body after thirty years and still not a pot to piss in," Brian exclaimed. "Sing your song all you want to the Canada day parade and to the newspapers, cause they're the ones who wrote the tune, but buddy if I have it good now hang me before things get bad, the Oligarchy will have everyone as mindless slaves soon enough"

"You've had some really crappy breaks I must admit, but in general Canada has it pretty good," Jason said.

"No Jason they don't, the U.S with they're over valued dollar, have it pretty good if they are ambitious, but that will change when their dollar dumps," Brian said knocking on wood," but Canadians are just feeder fish struggling to get through. If you had money before nineteen eighty and owned a home, life would seem pretty good but if you started out from scratch good luck. You work with the public Jason they all play act that they have so much but what they have is debt. Our parents didn't live that way or our grandparents and our grandparents had one income, let's see anyone buy a house and keep a family on one income today. If things weren't getting worse in Canada you would be able to buy a house, feed and clothe your family on an average man's salary, you can't, so things are obviously getting worse every year, end of argument."

"Here he is let's ask Bjorn," Brian said as he stood and waved at Bjorn.

"Bjorn this is Jason the owner of this fine establishment and this is John my best friend. Guys this is Bjorn."

They all said their hellos and introductions.

"So Bjorn what do you think of Canada?" asked John.

"Canada is a very beautiful country it is very liberating to be able to walk outside, see the trees, the large lawns and the sky without having to look straight up." Bjorn said laughing.

"Living in my country is like living in down town Toronto everywhere in Trums. It is; glass, chrome and decorated concrete everywhere your eyes can see. We have gardens with trees, but they are all gardens, enclosed and tended by gardeners not like here were the trees and grass grows on their own accord, free to sprout up anywhere it likes," Bjorn said describing the city of his birth.

"So do you like it better in Canada than in Aronia?" Jason asked.

"Canada has been very good to me and my family, the same as Aronia, but others have it so much harder here than in my country," Bjorn explained "Take the people Brian works with, they work every day and have nothing, they can't afford good automobiles yet they drive every day. If they buy a house they all of a sudden start working overtime every night and don't take their vacations instead of enjoying their families and their new homes. If they miss a day's work it takes them weeks to catch up on bills, if they miss two days they have collection guys calling them all day. They work every day getting farther in debt till vacation pay comes then they try to catch up. They have no life but work and bills."

"Well they have to work in Aronia as well don't they?" Jason asked.

"Yes everyone works or is in school, we haven't anyone that does nothing like here," Bjorn answered.

This was not the answer Jason was looking for and John started laughing at Jason's reaction which was caused by the innocent and sincere way Bjorn had answered Jason's question.

"Well in Aronia what if you wanted to own and run a coffee shop, let's say?" Jason asked.

"You can't own the café in Aronia, but you can manage it and people do. We all own the Café and that way the coffee is less expensive and everyone can afford it," Bjorn answered "We have café's very similar to this style, some have live music, some have computers to study, others are set up like libraries with books and big table, so like you, we can discuss intellectual matters."

"But you can't own it, doesn't that bother you?" Jason asked trying to make Bjorn understand the injustice of it.

"I told you, I do own it as does every other Aronian equally. Why would I want to own it by myself when I already get my coffee at a cheap price?" Bjorn asked.

Jason's expression went blank and he said "You just don't understand the pride of ownership."

Brian laughed ecstatically and whispered to John "Jason's mind has reached the edge of his box, now he must justify his lack of comprehension by thinking that it is Bjorn who cannot understand or his mind will be lost forever in the endless blackness of thinking 'outside the box'."

"No I guess not, I own a home here, well the bank does, but I had a home in Aronia, I appreciate the space and yard here but it is no more practical than what I had in Aronia, difference being everyone has a home in Aronia." Bjorn said not really understanding the concept but realizing that ownership was something that Canadians feel pretty passionately about.

"What are you two laughing at?" Jason yelled at Brian and John.
"Nothing, just that it's like your whole world just came crashing down on you that there's a whole society that doesn't dream of owning a Coffee Pub or that there's a whole society, that all have Coffee Pubs and couldn't care less," John said.

Jason thinks about the statement for a while thinking that he hadn't notice that there would be two sides to the equation.

"So you didn't find that you lacked the freedom in Aronia that you have here?" John asked.

"No, here the freedoms are very expensive and few can afford them where in Aronia everyone has the same opportunities. The one thing that's better is you can have as many children here as you can afford with no restrictions, which is wonderful, yet very few use it?" Bjorn said inquisitively.

"The ones that can't afford it are the only ones having children!" Brian said resentfully.

"Yes your people seem to allow and support a degenerating evolutionary cycle, why? Bjorn asked puzzled.

"Canada's; population problem, our degeneration problems, scholastic problems and school funding could all be solved with one word being changed in our taxation system. "Brian stated.

John started laughing and asked "Oh it's that easy one word and you're going to fix all of Canada. I'll bite what word?"

"Change credit to deduction." Brian said. "If you made a child tax deduction, where those who make a contribution to Canada, the people with the most drive and determination could deduct each child till at ten children they only paid five or ten percent of their income to the government they would reproduce like rabbits. If some C.E.O making forty million a year, obviously with a relatively high I.Q and education, can clear thirty six million of it and save himself sixteen million bucks a year you know he's having ten children. You know his children are all well-nourished and are learning drive and determination at home. He will adopt if need be, to get up to his ten children, which means any children that are not getting proper care now will get to live a life that would of never been possible before, no more foster homes. If you make legislation stopping private schools these guys are not letting little Johnny play football in crap equipment or read from ripped up old textbooks so part of his sixteen million goes to schooling donations. He is also making sure the education level is up to standard, so you get rid of the bush league teaching staff and make the educators work harder and more diligently at their art, just to keep their jobs. That means my kid gets all the same benefits with me making forty thousand a year."

"If we must live in a Oligarch or Capitalist society let's make it work for everyone, one simple change and we relieve poverty we increase our population with more adaptable children without importing millions of foreigners and we start a cycle that makes Canada more intelligent and more productive without giving up anything," Brian finished.

"WOW, where did you come up with that one. I have to admit it's genius" Jason said astounded that something like this hadn't already been done and that a nutbar like Brian was the one who came up with it.

" Yah it's pretty smart I got to admit but what politician is going to stick out their neck and make a motion that appears political incorrect and it would look as though the government is picking on the underprivileged," John said.

It helps everyone, who works and contributes to our society, my kids get better books and education because of it, my taxes end up going down in the long run, the wealth gets sped around and I would be able to have two children comfortably. It's because people who want to get ahead need two incomes coming in that they can't afford their wife being off every year pregnant. To get ahead you need capital and children draw a lot of capital right at the age couples need it the most. Welfare people have no plans of getting ahead, they don't need capital and they have lots of time on their hands. They also make more money if they have more children, under the current system, so who is being unfair to who?" Brian said getting in a furry; saying it loud enough that three people he was quite sure were on welfare could hear him.

Jason looked over at the three people and tells Brian to "shut up".

Brian laughed "funny that you would pick those three out, why? If you hadn't known what I was doing and you didn't know which people I was hoping to shame into contributing to our society, you would have a point, but since you do, I know you are in agreement, thank you, but political correctness insults your intelligence Jason."

"It's not even welfare any more Brian the government has made it a pension for the too lazy or too stupid to get a job, so they don't even know that you're talking about them, they are on a pension, they're not welfare, it's much more respectable." John laughed.

"This is the thing that I don't like about your country. You have the filth rich who control your government, the down trodden that do nothing, because they are ignorant and can't perform the tasks and then the vast majority that are in the middle that work and struggle to pay the way for both. Why do you allow this? It is a democracy and the majority should live the best." Bjorn sayed.

"Most are under an illusion that someday they will be in the filthy rich category, they all think they are going to win the lottery one day." Brian laughed.

"It's because it isn't really a democracy Bjorn it just takes the appearance of one. North American and most of the world has been under an Oligarchy that's been growing stronger since the nineteen twenties. They use the deception of a Democracy to keep the peasants in line and keep them from revolting against them." John explained to Bjorn.

"That's why they have worked so hard at destroying conscious thought in North American and why they are pushing for a world economy, so that they can solidify and expand their control. If they get a North American currency they will gain complete control over North America if they don't already have it. The only way to take back control from this super rich, super powerful family would be to implement a Consensus

Democracy and that won't work now because the people are not smart enough to make conscience decisions and will believe the television and press. Now the Oligarchy group control the press and television they can control a Consensus Democracy as well. They have won and all of mankind has lost," Brian added.

"This is what I have noticed" Bjorn replied " Monarchy's like ours and Autocracy's work well if the one who rules has a good heart and loves his people like in Aronia. But if corruption enters the picture things can go very badly, very fast in those systems of government as well."

"Why has that ever happened in Aronia?" Jason asked.

"No it has not, thankfully. The people feel protected because a good man has taught his sons and daughters to be good as well and to know the value of their people. There have always been the Royals who have always been involved in the political structure and they would intervene if a King did go astray. That is why Aronia is not happy that King Dominique has only had two children, it takes away the safe guard. Cuba now faces the problem that Fidel Castro is aging and the people are unsure whether his successor or the successor after him will be a just man of good heart like Castro. Cuba is very well educated, because of this they should be able to set up a stable system. The American sanctions and other world factions contribute to a problem of instability and whoever replaces Castro will have to be a great leader with the intellect of Castro."

"Aronia would be very hard to corrupt because the military is small, very well educated and has free will. They take their orders from the King but also from the Royals. If there was ever a tyrant King the military would know whose orders to follow and those would not likely be those of a tyrant. You know your leader is good and just because all I have said is in books and in the newspapers in Aronia. An unjust King would never let that be published" Bjorn answered Jason.

"That's like Thomas Jefferson when he wrote* "…wherever the people are well informed they can be trusted with their own government; that whenever things get so far wrong as to attract their notice, they may be relied on to set them to rights." Now there's a guy a leader doesn't want writing his speeches if he plans on oppressing a nation." Brian laughed.

"Do you always have to quote Jefferson?" Jason asked

"Jefferson and Carter were the most intelligent Presidents the United States have ever had, would you prefer me to give you a Bush or a Regan quote" Brian laughed.

Bjorn waved as an Aronian family walked into the Coffee Pub for ice crème and coffee. Brian, Jason and John turn to see who he was waving at.

"Are all Aronian families that large Bjorn?" John asked seeing that the young couple is pushing a double baby carriage and a stroller.

"Yes, it is a symbol of your success and your contribution to your society. I don't understand why Canadians don't do the same; your country has plenty of space for many more children. Don't you like sex?" Bjorn said then laughed.

"Yah, just don't get any" Brian chuckled.

Chapter X

Erikson Expedition

Peder and The whole Erikson family's training was supervised by the best minds and greatest teachers in all of Aronia. The birth of their son Dominique Erikson was a momentous occasion and though the family was allotted all the time they would need for the celebration of Dominique's birth they were already deep into learning English and French.

Peder was working harder than any one. His studies were much more intense with Canadian law, business, history, geography, accounting and social sciences. After he had mastered those which he was already well accustomed too, by working with North American trade for years, now he was put into a special geology course for mining and exploration. He had six weeks to learn what had taken others years but he had the advantage of having the best personal teachers teaching him. Peder soaked up every bit of the information. Tools that he was going to be accredited for inventing and methods that he was going to be accredited for developing he could recite or build in his sleep.

The importance of Peder's task and the incredible need to live up to and exceed King Dominique's expectations made Peder a very focused astute student and he soaked up information like a sponge. He demanded to write the exams that would have been given to the university students graduating the course so he could see how close he was to a standard he had set in his mind as what would be needed. He would have graduated with honours if he had of actually been going through to be a geologist. This left those around Peder, teaching him astounded and Peder satisfied, it was better than he had hoped, he had set the goal of being able to pass the final with at least an eighty percent grade.

Peder was teamed with Hall Steinn and his apprentice Geir Sigurdur. Hall was responsible for most of the innovative equipment used in the mining Industry most of which Peder would be taking credit for. It was said that Hall could sense a vain of minerals two miles down on a Sunday walk in the park. He was the best in Aronia probably one of the best in the world if not the best. Hall taught Peder everything he knew. He taught Peder when to spend the money going for the minerals and when to walk away and look elsewhere. He explained the option of walking away had ended on Vinland Island but there was hope that there was another area that was raised well up from the ocean shore that maybe prosperous.

Peder leant to be able to read core samples and seismic readings but Hall could tell things that weren't in the textbooks about core samples and seismic readings. He could tell by experience that by going this many degrees to the left or right the vein of ore would be wider and Peder had caught on to his little tricks and techniques, he was no Hall but he could pass.

The university that Peder attended was on Vinland Island as was the mines that he would be trained in. Vinland Island was a very long Island that was shaped like a crescent moon curving around the volcanic Islands. It was about five miles from main land Aronia and a mile from Tor a small volcanic Island used for farming. It was a long Island that gradually ascended into a mountain about eighteen hundred feet up.

The Island was relatively large being twenty miles long but only averaging about one mile wide. It had a large fortress and a small harbour that was originally built by the Spanish conquistadors. Around the fort was the town of Biorg where the; farmers, miners and the packaging plant workers lived. It was also the home of Mikkel the Kings brother and one of the Royals, who all in Vinland, respected, but none more that Hall.

Up the mountain grew the grapes that where alleged to be on vines fifteen hundred years old and the grape were the source of some of the finest wines in the world. The rest of the Island was all; farm land, orchards and pasture land for livestock, a small farming town and the opening of the largest mine in Aronia. It was the only mine that produced; Copper, steel and coal depending on which direction they mined.

Vinland Island was the only non-Volcanic Island in the group It is believed that hundreds if not thousands of centuries ago Vinland was likely part of a small continent that was destroyed by the volcano Oden. This would explain the shallow depths of the ocean around the Aronian group of Islands and this fact is what led Hall to believe that he could find much more minerals beneath the ocean. He felt that the land mass that was once there buried by ocean and volcano still had many minerals to supply Aronia.

While Peder was training to be a miner and a rich industrialist the Erikson Family was training in the art of being a rich Canadian aristocratic family. The children still attended school but with private teachers in English and French. Margot wanted to help by bringing her computer skills into the effort. She started designing computer programs that could help with the community that would be set up. The stats of all the Aronians in Canada and the positions they held that could be updated and accessed via the telephones andcompures. She designed a social networking system that with the use of the new internet system all the Aronians could use each other to network themselves into the best positions at the best jobs.

Margot and the Queen spent a lot of time together going over social parties and social norms of the elite Canadian wife. Margot commented to Queen Vivian that what she was teaching her was essentially how to be one of the North American soap opera characters. The Queen told Margot that it was a stroke of genius and the Erikson family watched soap operas all day long. This drove King Dominique and Peder insane.

The Eriksons spent the last three weeks living at the Royal mansion. Peder and the King went over the steps in the plan and the protocol in relaying information on updates. The Women and children watched soap operas off of the satellite. At super time and diner time the women and children would talk constantly about mindless babble of American propagandist garbage. The King told them that you must realize soap operas are one of the tools used to brain wash the North American people. When Peder and King Dominique went to observe the rubbish the women were watching, they couldn't believe the stuff on these shows, all these rich people who didn't seem to do anything for a living, waitresses driving hundred thousand dollar vehicles and living in four hundred thousand dollar houses. They watched the next two days just to try to understand the meal time conversations. During the last week of training nothing got acomplished because they were all sitting watching soap operas. "Powerful brain washing tool they have their," King Dominique said to Peder "I'm afraid I am going to have to remove the satellite dish for a while."

"It may be the most dangerous thing you ever do as King, makes the plan look pretty safe now," Peder replied.

At the airport the King and Queen and the Erikson's family gathered to say goodbye. Queen Vivian and Margot cried and hugged and hugged and cried for an hour. Margot's parents were wishing the children farewell and were overwhelmed at meeting the King and Queen. Peder's Parents could not hold in how proud they were and told Peder to have lots of children so they could visit each year.

The King gave Peder a going away present of an Oniax watch that Aronian made to compete with Rolex. It was a large gold watch with a thick crystal glass face and diamonds encircling the entire face, it kept eight different time zones; one was set for each of Canada's six time zones, one for Aronia and the last as Greenwich reference. On the back was inscribed "To a Great Aronian and a Great Friend from King Dominique Olafur IV and family." Peder lost himself and hugged the King. King Dominique gave Peder a bear hug that almost knocked Peder out and laughed as he said "Fair well my good friend. I will miss you, but we'll talk soon, after you get to your new home."

Queen Vivian took Margot to the side and said "Here I want you to have this, it will be something none of those snobby upper class women you will be having tea with can ever out do. It is the Diamond necklace King Louis the Sixth gave King Dominique the first's wife Queen Nanna, it's priceless and I want you to have it. I want you to call me all the time from the embassy and I'll call you at home from some anonymous number. Hopefully we will see each other at functions."

"Thank you so much, I have never felt closer to anyone in my life than you Queen Vivian. I hope this is not a dream because if it is I never want to wake up" Margot cried.

"Go on get on the plane your adventure begins." Vivian said slapping her on the buttocks.

Saying goodbye to Aronia was hard Margot tried to hold back the tears and to be strong for Peder and the children. The plane taxied down the runway and took off into the sky a tear trickled from the corner of Peder's eye. Margot said "Don't worry Peder it is going to be a wonderful adventure and we will have a great life, we can come back to visit all the time. "

Peder watch the island grow smaller and smaller till he was able to see the entire thing. Like a picture the great volcano Oden looking as though it was made by the Gods with green steps running up the sides of the great greyish blue mass, the steam coming from the opening at the top, looking like a Halo encircling the great Oden the lush green forest encircling the mountain with a steam running down the center falling down a wondrous waterfall to the great lake. The lake surrounded by forest and the forest protected by the great city of Trums the place Peder had called home his entire life.

As the Plane lifted higher and higher the smaller Islands came into site with Vinland surrounding their edge like a green fertile shield protecting the Islands from the east wind. Peder said to Margot "You don't realize how beautiful it is until you're up here leaving do you."

Margot who had been sobbing on Peder's shoulder watching out the window said "Just imagine how beautiful it will look when we see it coming back knowing that we had a part in helping her retain her beauty forever."

The flight was exciting. The children had never flown before so this was the experience of a life time to start the experience of a life time. After an hour of seeing nothing but endless ocean and not a trace of land anywhere the horizon became filled with dark land covering its length. As they got close the shine of a giant city on the shores came into view. The children all ran across the plane to see it yelling 'is that it, is that Canada?'

The pretty stewardess in the blue jacket and skirt tells the children "No children that's New York City in the United States if you look hard you can see the statue of liberty, there, it's so small from up here you can hardly tell but someday when you do get to see it she's beautiful. Toronto Canada is just a little bit further."

Shortly after the pilot announced that they were starting their decent to Toronto Pierson International Airport. The children got so excited and Margot and the stewardess had to get them settled down and in their seats.

Margot turned and looked at Peder and said "Well you ready to start our life as rich aristocrats" laughed and gave Peder a kiss.

Two years ago the term rich to Peder meant having a good life and a large loving family and he had already felt rich his entire life. Now the term was dirty in his mind it meant; money, power, control and feeling better than those around you. He thought 'if I accomplish nothing else I want to make at least one North American understand the meaning of rich'.

After seeing their little Island and knowing the problems they faced their, Peder looked out the plane window and couldn't believe how much space these people had and how little they utilized it. Land as far as the eye could see. The Idea of having to find resources here was looking a whole lot easier to Peder now that he could see the area he had to find it in. He thought that every inch of this untouched land must contain minerals and all this land must contain more than a thousand times what my little Islands could.

The land looked grey and harsh as they approached but as they got closer the glimmer off the ground became cleaner, brighter and then a beautiful white sparkling earth for miles. The white snow was everywhere, Margot and the children were so excited. Peder couldn't help but notice how different the place was than where they had just left. Giant highways full of automobiles spanned everywhere, small one and two storey buildings scattered the landscape sporadically and then grouping more tightly as they approached the airport. Peder knew this was caused by the fact they had so much space that utilizing the land in a productive efficient way was of no concern to them.

After landing the Erikson's made their way to the terminal to get their luggage. The airport was packed but the Erikson's didn't notice it was pretty normal for someone from Aronia; crowds were part of everyday life. The site of so many different coloured people all dressed so differently huddled together moving through the crowd in small groups.

It was like small unattached islands floating with one direction in mind manoeuvring around the currents to keep from colliding with other islands all going in different directions. One group would be darker skinned women wearing beautiful long bright coloured dresses and scarves over their heads and the men wearing long one piece garbs and turbans, another group wore oversized sport out fits with team names on them that looked five sizes too big. They were obviously not a team because they were horribly over weight and wore different team names, Peder was sure that this must be a fashion statement. There were; hats, veils, turbans, dresses skirts blue jeans even toga's all moving together in groups, in different directions.

The site of all the different groups wearing different styled costumes which was obviously because of different cultural beliefs and fashion tastes made a colourful and fantastic impression on the Eriksons.

Getting their luggage was the first dilemma Peder faced in his task for the King. The luggage came down a ramp and onto a giant silver moving sidewalk that carried the luggage around and around. Herds of Aronian students and immigrants flocked to the travelling luggage like cows to a mechanized feeding trough. Peder couldn't even remember what their luggage looked like and all the luggage travelling on the giant feeding trough looked the same to him. Margot said, rushed by Peder with Octavious pushing two big carts, "what are you waiting for Peder get the luggage" she cried.

Margot started pulling bag after bag off the luggage trough and tossing them to Octavious who would put them on the trolley. She had tied neon green ribbons to all the luggage that belonged to the Erikson's. "Not that one Octavious the ones with the orange neon have our winter coats in them," she said.

After getting all of their luggage on the cart with the ones with winter attire on the top, the Erikson's moved quickly through the crowds and through customs and immigration. There standing in the giant terminal building stood a man with a big placard reading "The Erikson Family".

Peder called out "over here".

The two men addressed Peder "Mr. Erikson welcome to Canada your business associates are waiting in the car and we have a limo van for the children to ride in. please follow us."

The two men took the carts but not before Margot had grabbed the winter clothing. Margot bundled the children in sweaters, snow suits hats and mitts. Peder was handed a thick blue trench coat that weighed a ton, a scarf and a pair of insulated leather gloves. Margot put on a parka and a scarf and rapped the baby in a blanket in the stroller making baby Dominique looked more like a fragile package zipped up in bubble wrap.

The Eriksons were taken to a long black limousine and a tall black Mercedes micro bus parked right outside the airport doors. When the doors to the airport opened and the cold wind hit Margot's face Margot exclaimed in shock to Peder. "My God Peder it's cold here"

"Don't worry Margot not for much longer it should be nice by the end of March, and I want to make a snow man with the children first." Peder laughed as he swished around in his trench coat trying to stay warm.

The two men opened the doors of the vehicles for the children, Peder and Margot.

"Here I'll put the baby in the car seat in the van." said the driver of the van.

"No Dominique will ride with us on my lap." Margot said.

"Mrs. Erikson I'm afraid that's not legal here "said the driver.

"If Mrs. Erikson wants to take the baby with her in the limo she will do so" instructed Peder playing his role as he was instructed.

Margot looked at Peder; she had never seen Peder act like that. He oozed of confidence and authority and looked at the driver as if he had done something despicable as he said it. Margot would have thought that she would find what Peder did as rude, but she didn't, as a matter of fact she found it very appealing and attractive. She was totally turned on and she thought that playing these characters with her double-O- seven may have benefits she hadn't even thought of.

"Yes Mr. Erikson as you wish," said the driver

When they entered the limousine two men in business suits and trench coats over their laps greeted them, stood slightly and shook Peder and Margot's hands saying "Welcome to Canada Mr. and Mrs. Erikson," they said in Aronian

"Thank you very much," Margot answered back in Aronian

Peder looked at Margot and then answered the gentlemen "Thank you glad to be here." he said, in bold English.

"Merci, Parlez vous francais?" Margot said in nearly perfect French, knowing that Peder's French was not as good as hers.

"Oui Oui Madame" both men said in unison.

"I am Frid Gunner and this is Geir Sigurdur." Frid said.

Frid Gunner was an expert on; world banking economics, business and investment banking. King Dominique had told Peder about Frid and said he was to be trusted. Frid knew the whole plan and part of that was going to make him a very successful banker if all worked out and for the plan to work out it needed a very successful banker.

"Hello I am Peder and this is my wife Margot, pleasure" Peder said shaking Frid's hand again.

"How are you doing Geir, liking it here?" Peder asked knowing Geir from his training.

"It's cold but the mining industry here is so immense and there is so much left undiscovered," Geir answered.

"Well that's what we're here for." Peder said obviously wanting to get right down to business.

Frid sets a brief case on his lap dials in the combination spins it around and slides it to Peder's lap. Peder opens the brief case asking "what's this?"

"It's your; Visa card from my bank, bank books, transfer slips for the funds put in your account from Aronia, cheques, phone book with all the names and numbers of the consortium members and a cell phone. My and Geir's numbers are in their as well with the ambassadors private number, immigration lawyer, lawyer and Prince Val's cell number when he is in the America's," Frid explained.

"I used to make these in Aronia for the cell phone companies, wait till you see how small they will be getting," he said holding up the large cellular phone.

"You will have to use land lines when you are touring the northern mines there is no reception where most of them are." said Geir

"The information on the mines?" Peder asked.

"At the house in your office" Geir replied.

"The furniture and the beds for the children?" Margot asked.

"The home is decorated in everything you and Queen Vivian picked out of the catalogues in Aronia Mrs. Erikson. My wife said that the house is much to empty, not homey and personal enough. She said that you and Queen Vivian couldn't have visualized how large the house was while you were picking out the décor, so she has planned a big shopping spree for you and her tomorrow if you would like? Frid answered.

"Marvellous" said Margot.

"Shopping is a female national pastime in this country." Frid added.

"Your office is set up as specified Mr. Erikson and we have a car for you at the house and a large van for family outings. There is an Aronian maid and nanny as well Mrs. Erikson." Frid finished.

"Oh, I won't need a maid or a nanny; I am fully capable of taking care of my own home." Margot protested.

"Mrs. Erikson you have not seen the size of this home and you will be very busy especially at the beginning. The Nanny maybe useful, you can always let her go if you don't need her, but it is what she is here for earning her immigration, she is also a teacher in sociology to help your family better understand the Canadian way of life. They are here by the Kings orders to help," Geir said.

"Very well" Margot relented.

"Mr. Erikson the King is requested that any calls to himself or the Minister be made by the embassy phone for security reasons," said Frid

"Yes I am aware, when can we look at the mines?" Peder asked excited to get to work.

"It is our and the ministers opinion that there is lots of time to get to the mining. The mine that looks the most promising financially to us is looking like it may be closing down because of the recession and the lower grade of iron ore that is produced there. Hall and I agree that the mine has significant amounts of high grade ore deeper and in the surrounding area and it is already set up for us. Our technology can process the lower grade ore cheaply and quickly, it is already better than what we are mining in Aronia," Geir said the passion obvious.

"But would their not be the availability to start a new mine with high grade ore with all this land to search." Peder asked

"Viability Mr. Erikson why pay to search when everything we need is right there and will cost next to nothing to be operational immediately," Geir stated.

"It's also political advantage Mr. Erikson, by showing up as the mine is laying off all the workers makes us hero's. The permits come easier the government red tape disappears. Its good public relations and it gets us in the industry with no questions asked," Frid answered.

"In the meantime we are going to work on making you a real-estate mogul. See there that large site of land to the left. There used to be industry all down there, closed down for years and there used to be a large transport company and there a brick making yard. You have already done soil sample testing and they are all willing to sell. The Paperwork's on your desk," Frid said.

"The giant sky needle, is that's the C.N. Tower?" Margot asked.

"Yes they are very proud of that in Toronto, tallest building in the world." Geir said.

"Are those living units beside it?" Peder asked.

"No those are all office buildings their housing units usual only go up twenty or so storeys here." Geir said.

"If they get that excited about a tower being the tallest in the world wouldn't one of our Aronian high-rise condos be a big deal here?" Peder asked.

"Well yes, it would be the tallest in Toronto probably North America. The famous and the wealthy would have to live on the top floor penthouse and the publicity would be huge Mr. Erikson."

Peder felt a bit uncomfortable being called Mr. Erikson all the time and he was about to say call me Peder when he realized that he was no long Peder, he was Mr. Erikson and the sign of respect by people calling him by such would be in line with his character, besides it was starting to grow on him.

"We have the blue prints, the engineering, all the specs and all the people who know how to build it. With no other building around like it you would have a view that would go on for miles. It would also take care of housing for six thousand Aronians and make them feel like back home. The Aronians that are going to move in can probably help build it and save us a fortune on labour costs" Peder said.

"That will definitely make a name for you in this town if we can get the permits." Geir said.

"That's what Prince Val taught me to do, with half the City looking for work and an Election fast approaching the permits should be easy," Peder said.

"There is every sign that the real estate market is coming back slowly so now would be the time," Frid said glowing at the idea he was involved with a project that would likely promote him in his bank.

"We don't have to worry about if the market is coming back or not Frid don't you get it, your bank lends me the money, I build the high-rise condo using Aronia people, then the Aronian Immigrants come to you for the mortgages and I fill the building at a huge profit. I pay back the loan you get promoted we use the profit to build community centers, the church and the schools. Tomorrow make the offers we have enough money in place correct?" Peder stated like it was nothing at all.

"Yes to buy the property but the costs of building the building, we are going to have to borrow or ask the King and we don't even know if we can get permission from the city," Frid said not used to moving quite so fast

"You let me worry about the permits and the permission," Peder said smiling

"OH MY GOD PEDER! Margot said in a shocked voice.

The estate was huge, a long twisted laneway led through giant oak trees to a four story limestone mansion. The mansion had a huge covered patio that spanned the center of the house for fifty feet jutting out from the house at the large double wooden doors to make a car port, so you would not have to get wet in the rain or snow coming or going to your car. The patio roof above the carport was a second story balcony with cast iron railing all around.

The driveway circled around a large fountain, passing under the carport at the front doors then led to three rounded topped double sized wooden garage doors. The roof of the Mansion was slate with coloured decorative red and green diamond shapes between the dormers.

The Mansion looked as though it had been built in the middle of a large park. There was a small barn in the back and large trees, with no leaves, scattered everywhere. Peder had to imagine how beautiful it would look in the summer.

When the car had stopped at the front doors Gerdur, Frid's wife opened the doors to welcome the Eriksons. They all introduced themselves and entered the house in awe. There were no thrones but Peder had half expected their might be, but the foyer was massive with a circular stair case running up both sides. To the left there was a large living room with a fireplace and rich carpets and a twelve foot ceiling. To the right was Peder's office and a billiards room immediately beside it. Farther back to the left was a large sunroom the led out to a giant deck surrounding the swimming pool. To the right behind the living room was a large dining room and straight in front of them was the kitchen. All the rooms where separated by sliding glass and stained wood doors except for the kitchen that had a normal wooden door.

The kitchen was all modern with; stainless steel and black gas stove, fridge and dish washer. There was an island set up in the center with a small sink in the middle and stools around the one edge.

Peder looked around and said to Margot "It'll do" then laughed

Margot was amazed by everything, she was told what it would be like, but she could not believe it once it was really happening. The children were lost in seconds running around the house finding their bedrooms. Mary had taken Dominique with her to explore and see their rooms. The children's voices echoed because like Gerdur Gunner had said the house was empty even though the Queen and Margot had thought they had bought everything out of the catalogue.

"I will take you to the Eaton's center tomorrow if you want some clothes and then we will hit the furniture stores and the art galleries, it'll be so much fun. I love the China you and Queen Vivian picked out but we need a fancy display case to show them off." Gerdur cackled.

"Where did you set up my computer room?" Margot asked.

"On the second floor, beside your bedroom, so you can look out and watch the children playing in the pool." Gerdur replied.

"Perfect" said Margot.

"Your husbands a brilliant man does he feel that his mining expertise and business knowledge can do well in Canada?" Gerdur inquired.

For a second Margot forgot that even the Aronians involved didn't know what was going on and that she would have to remember her role "Yes he is and yes he is very excited to help create a community that will benefit all Aronians here. The prospects of the mining industry look very lucrative in this country and he is sure to build a large mining corporation using his unique methods and state of the art equipment."

"That's wonderful. Frid was involved in buying and building the first church, seems weird calling it a church but we get to meet all our friends every Sunday and see how everyone is making out. We hold ceremonies for all the baby's welcoming them to the Aronian family and making sure all the families have everything they need, but we need a bigger church already or a couple of churches," Gerdur boasted.

After plans were made for a morning meeting by Peder and Margot's shopping spree everyone left and the Erikson family all sat around the hearth and talked about their feelings and what had impressed them most about their new country. After everyone had told their story it was time for bed. The children all went up to their new bedrooms and fell asleep almost immediately.

Margot, remembering the feelings that she had felt that afternoon when Peder had put the driver in his place, had other ideas about how to make their first night in their new country a day and night to remember. Peder seemed to share the same idea.

Early the next morning Peder went to his meeting with the members of the consortium. They started with the paperwork to make the consortium a legal entity and Peder went over his plan to build Toronto's largest high-rise condo skyscraper. Many worried that Peder was moving too fast but once Peder explained how it was the most viable way to start off, building what they knew with the people they knew from existing blueprints with existing engineering and the fact they had an automatic one hundred percent occupancy rate the consortium agreed and concurred with Peder's reasoning.

Peder contacted Prince Ivar to get him to send a scale model and the blueprints for the high-rise condo that would best fit the area. He asked for; the financials, projections, electrical plans plumbing plans everything he would need to start right away. He asked to be sent a list of all the most qualified people Aronia had sent to Canada to build the project. Peder asked if there was any way he could modify everything as to have a penthouse on the top floors and Ivar said it was easily done because North American Penthouses are not nearly as large as Aronian Eleven bedroom condos.

The next day everything was there, via the royal jet, Val and Ivar had come as well with a couple of their top people.

"Hello I didn't expect you to bring all this personally Ivar, but thank you." Peder said shocked.

Peder's office was on the top floor of a thirty eight story high-rise in down town Toronto. Frid had found it cheap for a high profile office through the bank. One of their customers downsizing and moving back to the States had walked away from the office. It had been furnished with desks and chairs, computers and furnished board room. Peder had a personal secretary named Grimur who the King had appointed as Peder's secretary in Aronia and was privy to the plan.

"We have taken what was the cafeteria and set up the models and the drawings," said Grimur.

"Thank you Grimur," Peder replied.

"We landed at six this morning so we had time to have it all set up for you," Ivar said glowing We have people taking pictures of the purposed site now so that we can super impose the building into the current skyline and surrounding buildings. Any Idea how many you are going to want to build? They look more impressive if you have sister towers.

"I was thinking one then another a little later on that way I will get the maximum rent for the lower grocery stores and retail outlets," Peder said.

"You should think about having Aronians run the stores no reason to let someone else in on six thousand potential customers all in one place," Prince Val said.

"Yes Prince Val I have considered that but I want to do a study on it to make sure it's my best option. I need to know if there are people here capable of running them and our own part time student trainees as labour will be fourteen years coming," Peder said.

"Quite right the equations do change a bit in a new land, but it's good to see that you're on top of it on your third day," Val laughed.

"Well here's your model equipped with two story penthouses ten in total. The top thirty floors are all five bedroom units the rest are all six and eight bedroom units. The mezzanine is on the twentieth floor and I have added round windows where our moving sidewalks usually exist. Once you build the sister tower you can add the bridge and it should be most impressive standing here side by side all alone." Ivar said very excited.

"Instead of having all the shops on the Mezzanine I think a gym and pool would work better here and widen the entrance so the shops can go on the ground floor, is that too much work and what kind of difference will it make in the cost of erecting the building," Peder said not wanting to offend Ivar but thinking that since most of these people live and are used to being close to the ground the shops should be on the ground floor.

"Your absolutely right Peder with only one building it is much more conceivable to have recreation on the mezzanine and the shops on the ground. Not a problem it can be done by tomorrow. "Ivar said

"Since I have you here and I might as well use you, how long would it take to have the pictures of the skyline the model complete with; subdivision, parking, little cars the whole nine yards as well as the numbers," Peder asked.

"It would take a week back in Aronia I will double check the list as to who I have here in Canada but I'm guessing I could have everything ready in a weeks' time, including substructure and Canadian code," Ivar said quickly doing the math in his head.

"Perfect, Grimur if you would fax the list to my home I'll have Margot input the information in the computer and get all the people that we need to put this thing up," Peder said.

"Mrs. Erikson doesn't have to do that Mr. Erikson we have excellent computer staff right here in the office," Grimur said.

"You don't know Margot she wants to do this, she has already made the program to be able to draw from any Aronian talent we have and have them called in a moment's notice. She would disown me if I allowed someone else to steal her thunder," Peder said.

What are your plans Peder from what we have heard from Frid things don't work that way here? You need permits and approval from three levels of government we were told that anything big like your high-rise skyscraper condos can take years," Ivar said.

"That's why I have Prince Val, Prince Val here, could sweet talk a pig out of her bacon, can't you Prince Val?" Peder said laughing "Or did King Dominique give me the wrong impression?"

"I cannot be directly involved Peder." Prince Val said.

"You don't have to be, just writing me up the presentation, talk about all the jobs the new look, the raised spirits this will bring to the people and how they will win the municipal and the provincial election because of it," Peder smiled.

"Wow Dominique was right about you if you want something done you're the man who can figure out how to do it," Prince Val said seeing a bit of himself and his brother in Peder.

"The Bureaucrats will want it done before the municipal election next march the provincial will want it roughly the same time, both are being blamed for the recession problems and they know housing is being stimulated by the fed so they can capitalise and take the bows as long as they have me to build them," Peder said with a widening smile.

"Can I have the second Tower and the walkway so I can add them right at the presentation? We need to put a nice park here that way it looks nice when there is only one tower and the spot is vacant when we're ready to build it?" Peder asked Ivar, pointing at the map.

"Yes definitely, with the penthouses" Ivar said.

Peder spent the next three weeks going to the most expensive restaurants with his new business partners, all the big benefits with Margot wearing the most expensive dresses. Wherever the Mayor was Peder would be there looking bigger better richer than anyone.

Frid suggested sending a bottle of wine to the Mayors table and Peder said "No wait till he sends one to us, everyone is dying to know who we are by now."

Peder was right by strategically being close enough to the Mayor at a benefit the Mayor approached Peder.

"Good day, nice get together. We haven't met, I'm Mayor Dick Petty and you are?"

"I am Peder Erikson, the mining industrialist and investor from Aronia. I'm here to figure out whether your city is viable for some real-estate investing I would like to do in my new country," Peter said as if the Mayor should have known who he was.

"This is my lovely wife Mrs. Margot Erikson" Peder said "Is your wife here tonight Mayor?"

The mayor nodded and called his wife over to introduce her. Margot immediately carted her off to go chatting and doing the girl thing.

"Let the women chat. I was eventually going to have to meet with you anyway, I have big plans for your city, plans that will make it the star of national press and get your people working and proud again" Peder said. "I'm going to need permits, zoning and the like but my plans are looking long-term and I am going to need to know where I stand with local and provincial governments and I need a stable government for the next six years to justify a risk of this magnitude.

"What are you planning Mr. Erikson?" the mayor asked.

"I will be having a little cocktail party here in a couple weeks when I am planning a press conference on my intention of building the tallest high-rise condominium building in North America to go along with your tallest building." Peder bragged.

"What I need to know is will you be running another term for Mayor and would you be planning on doing another term after that? Peder asked.

"Well yes I am running next election but five years from now I will have to see how the water feels before I go promising to jump in, but I am hoping." The Mayor answered.

"Have you ever thought about federal Politics…" the conversation went on for an hour by the time Peder left, the mayor had promised all the top spots at city hall, that where close to the mayor, would be honoured to attend Peder's party and press conference.

Frid bought the property and a month later Peder held a cocktail party at his mansion and had invited; the Mayor, the cities civil engineer, provincial members of parliament from the area, the premier, chief of police, city planner, bankers, C.E.Os of investment firms and the heads of the local unions. He also invited the top engineers that where in Canada from Aronia and all the C.E.Os from local construction companies and construction material companies. He had local sports heroes speak and hired a top celebrity to sing and a full orchestra to play. He had the models of the tower mounted in a gazebo with glass walls. The model of the tower and the community were all wired in so the complex would light itself, so they would all see what it looked like at night.

Peder would have everything he needed to start construction within two months. Peder felt that he probably didn't even need to have the windows broke out and the graffiti painted on the old factories and garbage placed about the intended site to make the eye sore he was about to clean up look worse.

Peder had realized from Margot's soap operas and the corruption that he read about in capitalist governments that it was the appearance of being a big shot and feeling like a big shot themselves that made people do things you wanted them to do. The fear of falling out of the spotlight and losing your big shot status was the other piece of leverage that gets you what you want if you can help keep them in there spotlight. Building the tallest North American high-rise brought with it a media spotlight that any government official would want shining on them, and Peder knew it.

Chapter XI

The Plan Is Coming Together

King Dominique sat in a board room with his family, these meetings were more common now and were separate from breakfast where they would discuss Aronian affair. These meetings where private and confidential, slowly more of the Royals would be participating in them but as of now only the seven were in the privy of the plan.

"What if it goes wrong on us Dominique, Castro was a hero, he had nothing but the best intent for his people but he was sanctioned and his people and his country have suffered ever since. He educated his people better than any other country except ours perhaps, he tried to run a system of equality like ours but the Capitalist run Government forces against Castro have hurt that country miserably. If the world looks unfavourable at what we are doing it could destroy us" Erik said, now understanding Dominique's plan and researching it in search of negative repercussions "the comparisons are unquestionable look at Iran, Iraq, Argentina the

Soviet Union they have all been devastated by holding on to their beliefs and defying the few capitalist that hold control. First they will vilify you and Aronia then they will sanction us. We have fifty eight million people to feed and keep; sanctions or the destruction of our monetary currency would hit us harder than any other nation. Look at what the United States did to Japan pre-world war two; an Island with limited resources doesn't stand a chance."

Dominique turned and said "We are doing nothing wrong, as a matter of fact we are being heralded as heroes by the world for our blending in and embracing multiculturalism. The Elite group that you speak about that would frown on this are content in thinking that their plan of infiltrating our country and getting to promote their interests is working. The system they use is self-propelled by simply allowing people to get what they want while accomplishing their tasks, sound familiar? Their unknowing soldiers won't know what buttons they're pushing or for whom. We have created a system that the people that unknowingly follow the directions of the Oligarchy are following the intent of our plan as well. I feel that our package is more enticing than theirs so their unknowing soldiers become ours. Time will tell who has the best minds and the best people. They are few and we are many it is the opposite of what King Domi was up against. Those who work for the Oligarchy's interests do so unknowingly and are being deceived, where what they are unknowingly fighting for is not in their best interests. What we are after benefits all except their elite few." The King said addressing Erik's and surely others in the rooms concerns.

"Do not underestimate the forces that will oppose us Dominique and do not overestimate the idea that a revelation will occur in the people being controlled by them. The people all think that they will someday be one of the elite few and dreams, no matter how impractically, are very hard to defeat. The Oligarchy probably run; the IMF, the most powerful banks and central banks, mining companies, oil co., and most of the world's gold and silver and like you they answer to no-one. I urge you to use very much caution," said Mikkel

"I am all about caution in our endeavour but the world reaction is wonderful, our people are being welcomed all over the world. Their productive qualities and their knowledge of their chosen fields are causing the world to beg for more Aronians for positions at their companies.

"We have emigrated over half a million Aronians around the world almost a hundred thousand to Australia and over two hundred thousand to Canada in just three years plus another Eighty thousand school Visa's to Canada. There has already been one hundred and fifty thousand Canadian born Aronians in Canada and the parents are as happy as any Aronian could be about raise their children there. Our people are happy, the countries and the people sponsoring them are happy, I'm happy let's not start worrying till there is something to worry about. Val said winking at King Dominique.

"The Treasury is being stretched worse than expected. We have over Twenty Billion vested already and have taken in only nine hundred million on the tuitions thus far," said Rolf.

"We had more students and emigrants than we had expected in the first three years. Everything is fine, our per-person budget is right on track, is it not?" said the King.

"Yes it is. I know that the idea of more immigrants is a touchy subject right now but the applications for student visas for our universities are growing significantly. If we permit more students to come here now that we have a system in place to amalgamate the foreign students in with our own, we could offset all the tuitions of our students going abroad and we would get ahead of our forecasts." Rolf said looking at Eir for her response.

"It is working out much better than I had expected, young adults have a tendency to adapt better, I guess, and the students are very helpful with programs for integrating the foreign students. The Aronian students have taught most of the foreign students how to speak pretty fluent Aronian. The German and Scandinavian kids had no problems right off the bat, catching on. The boy girl thing is a little sticky there is a double standard that does exist where the boys are dating the foreign girls but if the Aronian girls go out with a foreign student they are shunned, no one likes competition but I have personally addressed these issues and made it quite clear abstinence is a school policy here till your twenty three and married and the Aronian girls are putting their boys in check in this concern. We have a theft issue that we haven't had before and we have sent allot of student's packing because of drugs. The fact is I was expecting very much worse and my fear of this policy hurting the education received by Aronia students was misguided, if anything the education, by having them in our classrooms, may have proven beneficial." Eir responded.

"Over all it has worked out very well and I have no problem with you raising the number of available visas by thirty thousand; I believe that the foreign students are an educational tool for our students to better understand the world around them." Eir smiled at Leif who set up the integration process.

"We are having a bit of difficult satisfying those who have immigrated here. We have thirty three hundred immigrants from all different countries all older couples and some single males, all highly educated with no criminal records all over forty. Many of them have applied for family members to join them. We had made it clear right from the start that bringing family or friends to Aronia wouldn't be happening unless they qualified. They are having trouble blending in it would appear, mostly because of the lack of companionship we believe and the language barrier. Although the Aronian women and the people are nice to them and inquisitive about their lives in their home countries they are finding no companionship of a sexual nature because all our women of that age group are generally married," Erik reads from a study sitting in front of him.

"Five have been charged with rape, one drugged an Aronian boy and had his way with him! Mikkel screamed "do we just mark this down on a piece of paper as a casualty to our little ruse."

"Have they been tried or sentenced yet?" Dominique asked obviously upset.

"Their consulate is interviewing them and preparing for court, they want us to deport them back to their place of origin for trial. I suggest we take that route if possible, it will get us out of a bad situation." Val said with his head down speaking more as a plea than a suggestion.

"But they have committed no crime against anyone in their own country. They will stand trial here and will be prosecuted under Aronian law," said the King.

"That will cause a problem Dominique, the world knows that our laws, if convicted, the crime carries with it the death penalty, amnesty international is already here and is filing injunctions in the world court to try and stop the executions before it even goes to court," said Leif.

"Is there any question of their guilt? asked King Dominique.

"No, four have confessed upon capture the other has pleaded not guilty but the evidence is unquestionable as to his guilt," Leif replied.

"I want to see the victims personally and their families to beg their forgiveness, they are to be treated like no other Aronian and should never want for anything. This is my fault and I will not deny the responsibility. As well their attackers will be beheaded if found guilty and their embassies and Amnesty International may be there to witness it when it happens as will I. I will not feel responsible for any man's actions or lack of self-control and they will pay the price befitting their crime. If an Aronian did this to an immigrant the punishment would be the same, they have no one to blame but themselves. I blame no one for them being missed in the screening process but we must screen better and this must be screened against."

"Dominique the press is asking what they should print. They are afraid of causing turmoil and hatred towards the students and the immigrants," Val tells the King.

"As always nothing is printed about a crime till after the trial. As always I have no say in what they publish and make sure that is known, I however will comment on my decisions if asked. The victims' names shall not be released as well. Counselling and direction must be given to our people that every walk of life has it's good and its bad and nothing will justify violence or malcontent against anyone who had no part in someone else's actions," said the King.

"We should allow them mates Dominique," Mikkel said absolutely

"Allow our Immigration to permit women preferably of an older age Val this should suffice," said Dominique agreeing with Mikkel for once "but let's try and stick to older married couples in our immigration department shall we and the women we bring in for these immigrates to mate should be older than child rearing age."

'Yes Dominique but this is not going to go over well with the world if we start beheading their people. I would ask you to reconsider deporting them," Val begged.

"Val that might make our job easier, I will admit, but Aronia has so little crime and I must believe that has to do with the deterrents as well as the education and the system of equality. If we give up our beliefs in what made our nation great there would be no reason to proceed with our plan because we wouldn't be working to make things better we would be becoming the same. Let everyone know if you come to Aronia and you commit a violent crime your body will be returned in two bags," The King stated with a stiff upper lip.

Mikkel stood up from his chair and lifted his glass "To Aronia may our values hold fast to the goodness and the righteousness of man. Thank you Dominique I'm proud to call you my brother and my King."

They all lift their glasses in the toast but Val and Leif both look perplexed deep in thought on how to keep with; tradition, law, justice and not get wrapped up in world media backlash.

"It is settled then and I will prepare a statement to the world court telling them of our intent and our policy if the accused are found guilty," Leif said knowing that the Kings policy is going to challenge both Val and himself but knowing that it is right.

Dominique blamed himself for the victims' tragedy and would not allow himself to justify their suffering with the excuse of it being for the greater good. The woman of Aronia had to give up much to earn the trust of the Spanish in fifteen twenty nine and it was a shame that King Domi had to live with his whole life. King Dominique would have to show that kind of strength now because it was an uncompromising fact that the immigrants to Aronia where a necessary evil to achieve a utopia for all of Aronia in the future.

"I have good news we have even more Aronians that would be willing to immigrate to Canada after hearing from friends and family there," Erik announces

"Many Aronians have heard that there is less competition there for key positions in their chosen fields and the Agricultural industry have been told about all the unutilized space for farming. We also have many of our top executive positions that have read of Peder's accomplishments and would like to see how well they could do in that market environment. Their aptitude tests show a more ego driven reasoning behind wanting to go than others which would disqualify them under normal testing," Erik announced.

"Peder has talked to three of the Countries provincial leaders and if we would set up manufacturing facilities there in their respected provinces Peder said we could raise our quotas of emigrants to Canada with their immigrations blessing. Peder would like an answer so he can set up building housing developments in Manitoba, Saskatchewan and Nova Scotia. He has developed a list of products that we make here currently that because of shipping and access of building materials could be made their more cost effectively for the North American market," Val informed the group.

"Would this cost any Aronian their job here?" asked Mikkel.

"Not likely the list contains products that we can't currently compete with in the North American market," Erik answered.

"How many more Aronians would be allowed to emigrate and have jobs waiting?" asked the King

"About four thousand more than the government was previously permitting so we would be up over fifty four thousand a year plus the thirty thousand student visas," Erik smiled.

"Peder could use some help, have those executives apply and help set up these manufacturing facilities. Keep a closer eye on them, send the youngest with the least children. Give them less start-up money as well lets motivate their drive to succeed and tell them to see Peder if they get in trouble," the King granted.

"That Peder was the catch of a lifetime, give him whatever he needs and tell him to start building the new communities that he needs," the King said glowing.

"The execution thing may put a bit of a glitch in Peder's public relations as well King Dominique we must convey to him what is happening immediately," Val said "He is accomplishing everything quite quickly we don't want to knock the wheels off his cart so to speak."

"He has almost completed the first and largest community over there in Toronto and is being heralded as a hero for building the tallest condo high-rise in North America to go with their current C.N tower. The Papers are saying that he has raised the spirits of Torontonians to as high a level as the Tower itself," Val boasted.

"He has also stated that the building of the community is self-funded and very profitable and that Rolf could lower the start-up money because the government incentives for first time buyers have the bank pay for most of the house or condo and every Aronian has landed a well-paying position so far. He said every Aronian buying a house off of his company is putting fifty thousand dollars profit towards the next development. He said that the; schools the church and the community centers are all written off on taxes and cost nothing."

"This is great news, Peder is doing a wonderful job and the mining is on track as well I hear. You will see him for his grand opening Val , I would like you to take him a case of our finest scotch and wine for his big occasion to show our appreciation," The King said the pride he feels toward Peder obvious.

"I will, looking forward to it, I have prepared a speech for him to give at the gala and I plan on surprising him by giving it to him in person," Val said smiling.

"We meet tomorrow; I would like more on the trial proceedings, the steps that we are taking to alter the immigration policies to satisfy the single men with mates and older couples only. We must also discuss when we are going to reveal what is happening with the rest of the royals," the King addressed the table as they prepared to retire. .

Chapter XII

Brian Can't Catch a Break

His job was going nowhere and Brian knew it, he had to figure how to get out of Pre Fab Concrete Structures or die trying. Brian had developed so many make shift tools at Pre Fab Concrete Structures that you couldn't go through a day without using at least one of them. Then one day he was working with the crane, hooking up a concrete segment and the thumb of his glove got caught in the safety latch again and away went his torn glove up with the load. Brian knew it was more dangerous than just losing a glove some guys at work had lost their fingers and one had lost his thumb.

Brian went home that night and developed a device that would hook on to the back of the hooks and would allow the ground men to unhook the loads without having to put their fingers in the pinch point of the hook to release the safety latch. After building the device he discovered that with the device no one would have to work at heights releasing a load any more, they could do it from the ground by using an extendable bar and hook, to release the devise. He named it the saferclip and he patented it and took it to Pre Fab Concrete Structures to see if they would like to use it.

It worked amazing better than he had ever imagined, the device not only let you unhook the load it allowed you to pull the hooks free from the load as well so that the operator no longer had to manipulate the boom to do it. It also made it so that no hook up man would ever have to work at heights which would definitely save lives.

Everyone wanted the devices on the crane hooks except for upper management who wanted the saferclips on but thought Brian should have someone else manufacture them. The company searched for some other manufacturer to buy the saferclips from but couldn't find anyone. When Brian explained that no one else could have them for sale because he had invented and patented them, the management couldn't understand. The company couldn't comprehend that a real person could come up with something like that; some corporation must have it or something like it.

Brian found this to be true at most factories. The provinces agencies and the crane licencing agency both agreed Brian's device should be mandatory on lifting equipment but they couldn't make them law till they were actually available to the public and without hundreds of thousands of dollars Brian could not manufacture them in those quantities.

Brian tried everywhere to find a partner to manufacture the saferclips but he couldn't. The world's largest distribution company couldn't manufacture them but they were interested in buying tens of thousands of them to carry in there outlets.

Brian thought for sure that with an order that size someone would partner up with him or the bank would lend him the money. Manufacturing companies with the right equipment thought that they would be interested in a partnership as long as Brian paid them two hundred thousand for the moulds, punches and material to make them. When Brian explained to them that if he supplied the money for the moulds punches and material he would be buying the saferclips and he would receive all the profits they would just get paid, so they would be suppliers employed by him not partners. They didn't really understand that and things fell apart because Brian would usually treat them like the idiots they were. Brian was in disbelief that people of such low intellectual ability could ever obtain such high positions in the manufacturing business and after meeting many he was able to fully comprehend why all the manufacturing jobs were heading abroad.

John and Jason would tell Brian to just take them to the companies; it's a no brainer that they have to buy them. They would say how it increased production speed and safety, which Jason knew brought down WSIB rates. Little did they know that no-brainers were exactly what Brian was dealing with.

At the Coffee Pub that night the guys were talking politics and the subject seemed to be Bjorn and Aronia again because Pre Fab Concrete Structures was building a parking deck for Peder Erikson, a multi-millionaire from Aronia, who was building the tallest high-rise condo in North America.

"I'm telling you I think this is more than just joining the world community. Where does some guy in a socialist styled country get hundreds of millions of dollars to build super structures in Toronto?" Brian asked.

"Maybe he's Royalty the Saudi's built thing and own half the companies in North America, same thing," John said.

"We should ask Bjorn is he coming?" Jason asked.

"Yes, his wife just had number three and she's pregnant again. He has to let her get some sleep, three babies is a hand full." Brian explained "Three children in under four years is he trying for a record or something that's nuts and I don't even think it's healthy, "Jason said.

"That's what I'm talking about thousands of Aronians are coming here taking the best jobs and reproducing like rabbits, then some multi-millionaire industrialist shows up and starts buying half of Toronto. Don't any of you see a problem here? It's nice to have immigrants building infrastructure instead of running corner store or becoming phone solicitors but wow they're taking over," Brian ranted.

"Thought you would like that, thought you said they are the last hope for human intelligence," John said quoting Brian.

"Yes that's what I said and I still believe that the world would be a better place if everyone was like Aronians but I personally don't want to be run out of my own country just because I'm not Aronian," Brian said.

"You need to tell Bjorn that conspiracy theory, I wanna watch," Jason said.

Jason enjoyed watching Brian and Bjorn debate because they were both smart but Bjorn had much more finesse and didn't seem crazy like Brian. Everyone liked to watch Brian lose a debate but it didn't happen often because Brian and Bjorn usually agreed on matters.

"Doesn't matter they are doing more than their fair share of making the country a better place and there is a whole company that owes them the fact they have a job right now at Pre Fab Concrete Structure," Brian said.

"If you go on about immigration policies for an hour I'm leaving, you rattle on about it every day. We all agree with you even distribution and force them to develop infrastructure in areas that need development and not all herd to where they can just use our existing infrastructure. It's been tried it didn't work they all just ran away and headed to Toronto. But until your miracle one word fix the country policy is in place we are not populating our country ourselves so what can they do," John added not allowing Brian to get on the topic.

"How is the saferclip coming?" Jason asked

"It's not, no one will go into partnership to produce the damn things even though I have an order that will start me off with millions in profits" Brian said obviously frustrated.

"I don't get it" Bjorn said walking up to the group.

"Hi Bjorn" Everyone said greeting him as he walked up.

"I have seen how well the saferclip works; I can't believe no one has the foresight to see how profitable it will be to be part of the process. I know if you contact an Aronian company they will make it," Bjorn said.

"No I'm no Hypocrite, It will be made in Canada by Canadians or I will figure out how to produce it myself," Brian said.

"Well bring me one and the pamphlet on them I think I know someone in Canada that will build them and these people will believe me because I'm an engineer," Bjorn said.

"Great good luck, I need it," Brian said.

"So, Brian wants to know if he has to leave if Aronia overthrows Canada," Jason said trying to get a debate started.

"He can stay." Bjorn laughed looking at Jason insinuating that he would be kicked out.

"Why? I think we are helping your country very much, you think we should stop?" Bjorn asked.

"No it was me Bjorn, I was just saying, at the rate of reproduction your culture does and the fact that my culture doesn't that my culture is going to become extinct," Brian admits.

"Well go out and get laid, make a difference. Look at what you could be doing instead of sitting in here trying to solve the world's problems," Bjorn said laughing and giving a Brian a little kick under the table.

"I love your people but I'm worried about the cultural balance of the nation," Brian said.

"Don't worry I'll hide you guys in my basement," Bjorn kidded.

"So we were wondering about this Peder Erikson, what's the story on him. How does a guy make hundreds of millions of dollars in a socialist styled country?" Brian asked.

"Well I believe he is a lot like you Brian he invented a lot of very innovative mining equipment and the Royals appreciated it. Since he, like myself chose to come to Canada he was allowed the proceeds from his inventions and methods," Bjorn answered.

"So if he hadn't come to Canada he wouldn't have had the money he earned," Jason said getting back on his flag waving kick on democracy and capitalism.

"No he probably would have gotten a bigger place. For a contribution as large as his he would have unlike Brian been given everything he needs to keep him developing and prospering. They may have allowed him twelve children, the same as the Royals so as to hopefully give Aronia a few more like him in the future." Bjorn answered.

"Ha, bet he appreciates capitalism and democracy," Jason remarked.

"Why? So he can drive a nicer car than his friends?" Brian added.

"Well he gets to pick what car he gets to drive," Jason said not wanting to lose his point.

"In Aronia he wouldn't even want a car, Jason you are never going to understand," Bjorn said.

"Well you have to admit there is a bit of brainwashing going on in Aronia that makes people feel that way," Jason said.

"I think you have proven who has been brainwashed Jason, In Aronia we don't have to compensate for inadequacies by owning more stuff or more expensive stuff than our neighbours. In Aronia when we need something we know we need it and we go out and get it. In western societies you are told what you need through media and advertising so you feel you have to go buy it. What do you think brainwashing is? Bjorn said.

"Having to have an expensive automobile let's say a hummer and having to have a big house thirty miles outside the city, the media tells you this is a sign of success so you do it to impress people. Do you need a hummer to drive down the highway to the bank parking lot? People blame the snow to justify their purchase, I believe you had worse winters thirty years ago and everybody got to their jobs fine in cars what changed. The media told them they need a Hummer to look cool that's what changed. So who benefits from

people pretending to be successful in a leased,
because most of people can't afford to buy,
Hummer, in a five hundred thousand dollar home,
that they owe four hundred and sixty thousand on?
The oil companies, the insurance companies, the
government and the banks that's who. North
America is the most gullible brainwashed nation
in the world," as Bjorn makes his point Brian and
John laugh.

Chapter XIII

The Erikson Tower 1992

Peder had accomplished his first task for the King and had positioned himself for the rest of his mission. The role of multi-millionaire Aristocrat, Business mogul was easier than Peder had ever imagined. He had learnt the value of prestige. People granted power by government had a desire to be successful and look like they were one of the movers and shakers associated with big people. A handshake and a photo at a function could earn you a permit. Acknowledging someone at a restaurant and going over to their table may earn you a change to city ordinances.

The high-rise condo he had built had earned him a reputation that money couldn't buy. The big shot syndrome reaped huge rewards with every big shot executive needing to live above everyone else in the Penthouses. The bidding war on the penthouses between Toronto executives put the price at two and a half million a condo even though they only cost twice what it cost to build the units that he planned on selling for two hundred thousand dollar.

Peder said to Frid "Two and a half million dollars for a six bedroom condo just because it is two stories with vaulted ceilings and is situated above everyone else. These people are the least intelligent people I have ever seen, how did they ever get to a position to afford such extravagances?"

"And eighty one hundred feet above Toronto," Frid adds.

"All for prestige, it is insane. How shallow can a society get and how naïve," Peder said in awe.

"It works, look at you they have no idea who you really are or what talents you have all they care about is that you have a lot of money and that you're famous. It doesn't make sense people give their money to the guy with the best suit, the fanciest car and the biggest highest office to invest for them before they will give it to the guy in a reasonable suit a reasonable car and an affordable office. Why?, I guess they figure they want to make sure that he can afford another suit, car and pay the rent with their money. The fact that the other guy is actually investing their money instead of buying things for himself never occurs to them," laughed Frid.

"Take an Insurance company Peder, people don't trust themselves to hold onto and save their own money, so they give it to people to hold on and invest for them. Then they watch that company grow, building the most expensive office buildings, buying private jets and C.E.O paying themselves tens of millions. This makes them feel secure but if they handed a million dollars to their next door neighbour to hold on to for them and their neighbour went out and bought a new Hummer and a Porsche the next day you can bet they would want to see their money right away. These people are brainwashed and they will fight to protect the fantasy that has been put into their brain," Frid said with a grin.

Peder was sure he had made the King proud and Peder wanted to deliver the news to the King first. He had plans to visit the embassy that night to have letters delivered to the King and give him a call to let the King know how well things were going. Peder also wanted to tell the King how much he wished the King could be at the ribbon cutting ceremony with him to share in the success and tell him how much he'd be missed.

Peder's morning started out with a meeting with Frid about mortgages for Aronians who would be living in the bottom fifty stories of the new building and the sub division around it. They discussed repaying the loan to the bank and the ribbon cutting ceremony that night at Erikson Towers. Peder didn't like naming the tower Erikson towers he thought it was wrong to name the tower after himself. In Aronia it would have been just another high-rise condo but here it would be a landmark and Frid said it needed a name just like you name a ship. Peder thought the "Aronia" or Domi Park Toronto but knew that that would surely not work well in keeping his mission unnoticed. Frid wanted Erikson tower because he said money and power are all about ego and prestige and having a landmark named after you would give Peder a lot of pull with; government, banks and investors. Peder knew Frid was right seeing all the top people in the city and the province jockeying for positions at the ribbon cutting ceremony.

King Dominique had been leery about all the press and attention Peder had been getting. The King's original plan was to do everything in stealth with no attention drawn to their little endeavour. Frid and the Kings advisors all agreed that having the press and the public idolizing Peder as a business man was perfect because it put their attention on something other than the Kings plan and help to accomplish it. They could see how by using this to their advantage doors to government and Immigration would be opened and investors would flock to help pay for their obtaining the mines. It would be the Kings decision and Dominique's choice was to let Peder do whatever he felt would best accomplish what he had set out to do. He trusted Peder and Peder had over three hundred thousand Aronians there to back him up.

Peder had written the King telling the King that the vision that they had in mind was coming together faster than either of them had expected and that the press and the hoopla that these Canadians put on the wealthy was doing nothing but moving things along faster. He had wrote the King that the banks were calling him asking to open money lines for him, other cities were sending proposals for him to start developments in their cities. The mayor of Toronto and the Premier of Ontario would be cutting the ribbon with him at the grand opening of Erikson Tower. He assured the King that he would always be vigilant and cautious the plan would never be revealed.

King Dominique felt more at ease when Queen Vivian handed him a copy of the New York Times that read ***Aronian immigration pays big dividends for city of Toronto*** with a picture of Erikson Tower and a write up about the ribbon cutting that was to take place.

When the big evening had come, Peder went to the Embassy to deliver his letters for the King and to phone him. As he walked through the doors Prince Val walked up.

"I'll deliver those for you if you'd like Peder" Val said giving Peder a big hand shake as he took the letters.

"Prince Val what a treat sir" Peder said.

"I thought I would accompany the Ambassador and his wife to the ribbon cutting and crash your party." The Prince said grinning.

"No need to crash it, Prince Val you have my personal invitation and you may all ride with us," Peder said as he opens the door for Margot who is radiant in her gown.

"Margot my dear you look stunning." Val said as he moved forward giving her a hug and a kiss on the cheek.

"Prince Val I'm so glad to see you Queen Vivian and King Dominique aren't here are they?" Margot said looking around so excited to see Prince Val and hoping she would get to see Queen Vivian.

"No that would be a bit obvious, they send their blessings though and Queen Vivian says to call her tonight she misses you so badly," said Val

"Not nearly as much as I miss her. Will you be riding with us to the gala tonight Prince Val?" Margot asked.

"No tonight is you and Peder's night, the spot lights on you and we don't want to have this tied in any way with Aronia's Royal family so I will be just one of the crowd and please just introduce me as our friend Val, if anyone asks" Val said.

"You have done a stellar job here Peder the King is aglow when he talks about your efforts and successes. I have to admit my brother has an eye for talent," Val stated.

"Well thank you Prince Val, I'm doing my best and I have Margot, my family, Frid and all of Aronia behind me so how could I fail. All I did was say we need a building there, point and the best Aronians in Canada showed up and build it in Aronian time. No one here in Canada can believe how fast the building went up, everyone involved got huge promotions and have been offered top positions in other Engineering firms and construction firms all over North America. Frid expects that he is getting promoted right to the executive investment manager position once he walks in with a deal for the mines from our consortium and he is the one asked to handle the initial stock offering" Peder said modestly

"Margot I have a letter to you from the Queen" Val said pulling a letter from his pocket "and a case of Aronian scotch from the King for you Peder." Val said handing Margot the letter

"Really" Margot screamed grabbing the letter and ripping it open.

My Dearest Margot,

I am so happy for you and Peder everything is going so well for you. We saw your picture in the paper and you look amazing.

Your accomplishments over there in Canada has done me and Dominique a Great service , Dominique is so confident in Peder that he has Reassess his own personal life based on the final achievement that he is sure your family will accomplish.

I wanted you to be the first to know that the royal family is about to grow and knock on wood give their country a Princess. I am so Happy. Enjoy your Gala tonight, I wish I could be there as does Dominique. I would have liked to be able to tell you in person what you have given to me and my family.

Love Vivian

Margot screamed!

"What's the matter Margot?" Prince Val asked.

"Get me to that phone I have to call the Queen," Margot demanded.

The ambassador opens the door to his office and pulls the telephone to the edge of the desk.

"I was asked to make this call in private if you don't mind," Margot told the Ambassador, Val and her husband "Girl talk."

Val Peder and the Ambassador stood there looking like three men who had just been scolded by their mother. Standing there in their tuxedos looking like three lost penguins they look at each other wondering what and where they were supposed to do and go next.

"Out" Margot yelled as the men ran out of the office.

The baffled look on the men's face only got stranger as the shrieks and giggles from behind the doors echoed into the lobby.

"Real secure private office you have their Ambassador" Val said half joking.

"It's sound proof" said the Ambassador not believing the shrieks inside the room, his eyebrows raised making his forehead bunched up in wrinkles, hands opened facing up as he shrugs.

Ten minutes later Margot emerged from the office.

"Ok" boys, the King is on the line and he wants to talk to you, he has an announcement," Margot said glowing and flush from the excitement.

"Are you there Margot?" The Kings voice echoed as if talking through a tunnel on the speaker phone.

"Yes King Dominique they are all in the room," Margot replied.

"First of all I would like to congratulate Peder on the marvellous job he has done in such a short time and pass on the congratulations to Frid and everyone involved." The King said echoing over the speaker phone.

"Thank you my King it is my pleasure to serve." Peder answered

"Now I have a bigger announcement, Peder and Margot are expecting a baby girl if the doctors are correct and the ultrasounds are right, Congratulations" The King announces in a big proud voice.

Everyone starts shaking Peder's hand and wishing him and Margot congratulations, Val gives Margot a big hug as the Ambassador grabs three cigars from his desk.

"Hold on hold on listen listen" Margot said jumping up and down so excited she was about to burst. "Tell them tell them." she screamed

"More, what more could this glorious night bring," Val elates.

"Wait wait!" Margot screamed.

"Ok Margot, You gentlemen will be the first to hear, well second after myself and Maggot, that Queen Vivian will be blessing me and all of Aronia with a third child to the throne," the King announced.

The men cheered as the Ambassador poured the bottle of scotch that Val just pulled out of the box that he had brought for Peder from the King.

"Well congratulations brother and you too Queen Vivian I am so happy for both of you," Val said puffing on his cigar. "Tonight is by far one of the most exciting nights ever for Aronians around the world."

"Congratulation King Dominique and Queen Vivian you must be ecstatic," Peder said.

"This is thanks to you Peder that I feel secure in my choice to continue the Royal family and lay seeds for a prosperous future," the King said thanking Peder.

"Now I would appreciate it if you kept this hush hush until I tell the rest of my family and make an official statement to Aronia if you wouldn't mind. The Queen would like to congratulate you Peder and thank everyone for their support." The King said

"Congratulations Peder you must be very proud of your Margot and you treat her good and thank you everyone for your warm inspirational support," the Queen said.

"The greatest Gift an Aronian can give the world is an Aronian child," recites the Ambassador, changing the quote to the world instead of just Aronia "Long live Aronia."

"Long live Aronia" everyone said together, raising their glasses of scotch in the air.

The King thanked everyone for the warm wishes as did Peder and Margot then the King asked to speak to Peder alone for a while

"Yes your majesty we are alone now." Peder told the King as he picks up the phone taking it off of speaker.

"Peder you have exceeded everyone's expectations, the minister of finance said we better watch it or you will by the mines for yourself," the King laughed.

"My King everything that has been done here has been done in the name of Aronia and my King and only because of you has it come to be," Peder say honestly

"Peder your loyalty is the one thing that has never been in doubt not by me or Queen Vivian nor by the Royals," the King said in a softer voice.

"I wanted to congratulate you personally on everything and tell you how proud I am of you and your family, and wish you the best at tonight's grand gala," The King said excited for Peder.

"Thank you my King my only regret is that you can't be here to celebrate this with me sir," Peder said.

"Peder there is no need to call me sir just King Dominique, I seriously owe you more than you could ever imagine," the King said.

After the goodbyes the group left in separate limos to the Grand opening of Erikson Towers. They could see the search lights passing back and forth through the Toronto sky, coloured search lights rose up and down the building itself. The windows of the building were turning on and off one floor at a time going up to the top then down to the ground floor then all on at the same time. An Aronian electrician had suggested that it would be very impressive and wouldn't be hard to do and Peder had to agree the site was astounding.

When they arrived, the police escorted their limo through the crowd of onlookers, to the base of the great building, where many of the early guests had already arrived and hundreds of service staff were getting prepared for the festivities.

The spectacle, even though Peder had help arrange it, was more amazing than Peder could have imagined. A giant cake shaped like the high-rise sat in front of a head table, a giant Champaign fountain in front of the cake tower, built the same as the fountain in front of the real tower. There were clowns and clowns on stilts that were fifteen feet tall, jugglers, fire breathers and acrobats. All the servers wore grey server tuxedos that were more uniform styled so they could be picked out in the crowd, their trays were lit by glowing neon fibre optics. Peder felt that they really didn't need any help standing out because the Aronian students that were catering the event stood quite a bit taller that the guests that had already arrived.

"Next time make sure that I make the servers domestic Canadians, it looks bad it will give away too much and may make people ask questions if they're all Aronians," He said to Margot who is in awe at the spectacle.

Peder said to Margot "Aronians can really throw a party eh"

Margot laughed "You used "Eh."

"So I did" Peder said with a smile.

They made it to the front of the party in time to welcome; the Premier, the Mayor, all the local members of parliament both provincial and federal, the rich aristocratic from Toronto, the owners of the condos and the famous people who had attended.

After the Government people made their speeches welcoming Peder to Toronto and thanking him for blessing the city with jobs and this great building, it was Peder's turn.

Peder had never made a speech to a crowd this large and even though Prince Val had written it and had promised it would be well received Peder was nervous. As he stood up he thought this is all just part of the act, just business. As he walked up to the microphone he had developed his character in his mind and it was just play acting.

"Ladies and Gentleman, Madame et Monsieur's,

I am here tonight to give to the city of Toronto and this great Country of Canada a place for your people and families to call home. I have only lived here for a short time but the people I've met and friends I have made in that

time have made it some of the most enjoyable of my life. I made my fortune in the mining industry back in Aronia and came to Canada because of the vast uncharted regions of mineral rich land, hoping to make, well hoping to make myself rich is what I was hoping (the crowd laughed just as Val had said they would, Peder looked out grinning and laughed with them) but to make my friends richer the people around me richer and my new found country richer and a more prosperous place for everyone. (Every one applauded again as Val had said they would.)

When I arrived here in Canada I commented on the height of the city and the fact that it was beautiful to see the sky all around you as you walk through the big town. They asked me if the buildings in Aronia were taller than here in Toronto. I told him that the buildings in Aronia are much taller than here. Just my luck I would be standing facing him with the C.N. Tower behind me. (Again the crowd chuckled as was predicted by Val) He probably thought what a moron, are all Aronians this dumb. Then I noticed all of Toronto's tallest skyscrapers are office buildings. In Aronia this is not so, all our condos are as high as the skyscrapers and I thought what a wonderful view I could give the people of Toronto, what a wondrous gift I could give my new home, if I built a super structure condo here. With the support of the great people of Toronto, the help of your Mayor (turning and acknowledging the Mayor, the mayor stood up, bowed and then reseated himself) and your local government officials (they all took their acknowledgement) I give Toronto the tallest condo in North America ten feet taller than any in Aronia, but that was just and ego thing.

To my friend I met that first day, no still not as big as the C.N. tower, maybe next time (again the crowd laughed).

Before I forget, and boy you don't want to forget that one, I want to thank my wife and children for the support and love during the long unforgiving hours of work that something like this entails, Ladies and Gentleman my wife Margot Erikson (Margot stood up and radiated the crowd with her enormous smile and waved while Peder gave her a kiss and the crowd applauds) Who has just informed me that I am going to be a Dad again. Thank you Toronto Thank you Canada thank you everybody. I give you "ERIKSON TOWERS". (Fireworks go

off by the millions and all the lights flashed on and off at the end of the speech. The crowd gave a standing ovation as the band began to play).
Let's party."

Peder's first speech was a huge success, he made them laugh, he made them applaud, he filled them with Torontonian and national pride, but most importantly he made himself and all Aronians seem; human, compassionate and Canadian.

Val stood the longest applauding and giving Peder the thumbs up.

"That was a wonderful speech Peder." Margot said giving Peder a long loving kiss in front of a million cameras. "Did Val write it?"

"Most of it, I added the thank you, to you, the announcement of the Baby and the let's party bit," Peder confessed.

"Well then you are a genius" Margot joked.

The hobnobbing went into the wee hours of the morning. Peder had to do interviews with dozens of news media and got to meet the premier of Manitoba and Nova Scotia quickly discussing business.

The highlight of the party though had been Margot; she was the envy of every woman at the gala. She had been chatting with the Premier's wives when she introduced Peder to them and told him that they would like to talk with him. Peder had already been talking to both gentlemen but it was the first time they had met in person. Everyone warmed up to her and they all treated her like she was the first lady or something, and Margot shined.

Val cornered Peder getting him alone for a second and told him how great of a job he had done.

"I needed to warn you that the King intents to carry out Aronian law against the rapists in Aronia. This will hurt your P.R. here in Canada I am sure," Val said

"I don't think so the media won't cover it or blame any individual, they may try and use it to smear Aronia a bit but the majority of Canadians want the death penalty but their Government won't honour their wishes, so the media won't say anything because it will get the people debating on the subject instead of hockey," Peder said now starting to understand the relationship between Government, big business and the press

"Well be ready just in case "Val said

"I'll just tell them that if they are guilty good why feed and keep someone who is hurting their society and the people around them, they will never write that or show that on the news," Peder said.

"Tell the King it may be better to use lethal injection or something, beheading may stir the pot a bit," Peder said cringing at what Canadians may think of beheading even though the reason it was done was it was absolute, quick, and probably painless.

After saying the goodbyes and the servers started cleaning up Peder grabbed Margot and with; a bottle of champagne, a bottle of ginger ale and a comforter walked her into the great building.

The two story entrance was amazing all marble and glass with the shops up and down the corridors. Leather sofas with chrome armrests circled a small fountain and a glass encasement around the four elevators that stood behind the fountain. Two more elevators where situated at each end of the building as well.

Peder took Margot to the big chrome doors of the elevator and scanned his card. "What are you doing Peder, where are you taking me?" Margot laughed.

"Too the top of the world, baby, to the top of the world," He said in his best James Cagney impersonation.

After taking the elevator seventy nine stories the doors of the Elevator opened and they looked out at a private entrance with all marble floors with decoratively carved marble walls. Big double mahogany doors led into a huge two story vaulted ceiling open concept living room, dining room, and kitchen. Giant roman columns separated each would be room, the living room being down a step from the; entrance the kitchen and the dining room. The living room wall was all windows looking over the city to Lake Ontario. A floating stair case circled both sides leading up to a railed mezzanine with the bedrooms behind it.

"It's a building like back home but it doesn't feel the same as back home does it?" Margot asked.

"Well Aronia didn't shell out for vaulted ceilings and two story units," Peder answered.

"No I mean our buildings are this tall well ten feet shorter and they never seemed this serene and peaceful," she said.

"Well we don't have seven kids running around or the wall of the building next door to look at," Peder answered.

Peder laid out the comforter in front of the giant glass windows pulled out two glasses and the two bottles and poured Margot and himself a glass.

"Peter we can't do that who does this condo belongs to?" Margot questioned.

"It belongs to me until tomorrow," Peder said with a smile.

"Well in that case" Margot said lying down under the skylights looking up at the stars that twinkled above them.

"That's beautiful," Margot said looking up. "I would want my bedroom right here."

"It will be tonight" Peder said.

"You're so bad" said Margot.

"I'm happy" Peder replied.

"Yes the whole thing is going very well; the King and Queen are so impressed by what you have done," Margot said.

"I'm talking about you, I'm so lucky to have you and you giving me another child," Peder crooned.

Peder walked to the balcony "You know what the King told me that night, the first time we met?" Peder asked remembering back.

"What Peder?"

"He served me. He poured me a glass of Aronian scotch, I couldn't believe it."

"He Did," Margot replied.

"a couple actually," Peder laughed.

Peder was looking out over the city at the lights, the big black mass that was the Great Lake and down at the subdivision.

"He told me that I would know what it felt like to be him," Peder said.

"Do you know what he meant Peder?" Margot asked her voice soft and poetic.

"I do now, right now, for the first time. As I look out there and I see where I need to build more homes for Aronian families. I'm building jobs, careers, over there I should build a community complex and there an office building. I should set up a legal office for our consortium to handle our affairs and put Aronian lawyers to work. As they get bigger they will hire more Aronians and start taking jobs from other companies, and grow even more. They will grow by themselves to serve everyone all I do is get them started. I won't even know who works there; I just plant the seed for them."

"The King said that it feels like being a gardener. You plant the seeds you give them what they need to grow and flourish then you watch and if they need trimming from time to time you step in to trim but mostly, if it's been done right, you just watch it take care of itself," Peder explained.

"Well King Peder are you going to get over here and take care of your Queen?" Margot said seductively.

"Well we are going to have to hurry we have eight hundred other condos to Christen before the nights out" Peder smiled while slipping Margot's dress off after slinging his tuxedo jacket to the floor

"Oh Peder"

Chapter XIV

Brian's Big Day

Brian's turmoil over his Saferclip never seeing production ended with Bjorn's friends jumping on the chance to have a unique product to market. The meeting took place in Toronto and Brian was introduced by Bjorn as the genius behind the Saferclip.

They told Brian that they were willing to patent it worldwide under his name with their company as sole sponsors but for that they wanted absolute rights to produce the product and the consumable clips. They would pay for the different countries standards agency's approvals and they would also pay him fifty thousand up front to help with his legal and other expenses plus twenty percent of sales.

Brian had hoped for more cash up front but his provisional patent was about to run out leaving him no choice. Bjorn had promised Brian that this company would definitely produce and market his Saferclip with all their resources because they were Aronian and it just made sense if they want to succeed.

Brian took the deal and the fifty thousand covered what he had left of the legal expenses and bought him and his daughter a few of the things they needed and had gone without for too long. Most importantly it took care of all his debt.

They all laughed at him at work because he thought he was going to get rich off of the Saferclip and they had all said that he wouldn't get much that someone would steal the idea and make them and he wouldn't see a cent. Even though they were wrong about him not seeing a cent they felt a certain sense of being right by the fact Brian's millions turned into fifty grand.

"Well you got to be happy at least you got the patents, that was worth it right there and it will be made in Canada. I thought it would have been worth a lot more than that but it's just a start, right, "John said.

"Me too but I doubt very much if anyone else would have went for the twenty percent, so I am happy cause once they're set up and producing I will reap a far bigger reward from the percentage than if I had gotten a lot of cash up front," Brian said .

"Look at the good side maybe since you are working with the Aronians they will consider you one of them when they over throw Canada and you'll get to join them," Jason said laughing at Brian for his anti Aronian comments

"I never said they would over throw us I just said that we would be out voted and then we would have to assimilate to their ways instead of them assimilating to ours, its text book colonization ask the native Canadians," Brian said defending himself "I'm not even saying that assimilation to their ways is a bad thing but losing the Canadian Identity and being treated like second class citizens in our own country just doesn't sit well with me. They will want an Aronian state which means they don't really want me or my children here".

Brian continues "Listen that Peder Erikson just bought up one of Ontario's biggest mines for peanuts, he has started building the second tower and he's building communities right across Canada, it does look like they are following a colonization plan, hypothetically."

"You're nuts. Well first of all the mine was closing down he just felt his equipment could still mine the ore cheap enough to make a few bucks, let's face it Bjorn told us that was Erikson's background. Second if the building of these super structures was colonization wouldn't they be being lived in by Aronians. These places are big bucks, two and a half million for the penthouses and half a million for the normal condos. Nobody just off the boat is buying those" John explained.

"Got to tell you though there is a hell of a lot of them now, have you seen the church they built, it's like the size of the sky dome for God sakes," Jason said.

"That's because their people still go to church Jason if we all went every Sunday we'd need a hell of a lot bigger churches as well," John said.

"Speaking of the sky dome what do you think about the city of Toronto paying over six hundred million to build it and then giving it away to some rich jerk off for 25 million just so they can keep their ball team and he can make all the money selling the games to you on T.V," Brian asked.

"The people of Toronto should demand that they get to go to all the ball games free till their six hundred million dollar credit runs out." Jason protested

"Oh my god Jason" Brian said as he stood up and kissed Jason on the forehead. "I think I have broken through that thick capitalist skull of yours."

John started laughing his ass off as Jason was pathetically wiping the germs off his forehead and looking around to see who saw.

Jason started laughing "Ok, that was pathetic and the papers sell it like he did the city a huge favour and the sports fans don't care they probably think he's a hero for saving their damn ball team."

"Yah would have thought someone would have gotten upset about their five hundred bucks worth of tax dollars being given away to one of the richest men in Canada." John added

"Did you hear Bjorn is on number five, five kids. Do you believe it the guys only like twenty eight-years-old?" Brian exclaimed

"Yep I should have invested in baby food or a stroller company as soon as I met Bjorn I would have probably been rich by now" John said a little bit serious

"They come in here with a double strollers and a buggy almost all of them and the girls look so young to be having that many children" Jason said

"Well maybe Peder Erikson should have bought the sky dome for his church it would have probably been cheaper." Brian laughed

"Yea and on week days they could have little league games each team would be from one family." John laughed

Chapter XV

The Royal Get Their Mine

"Hello everyone" King Dominique said, addressing most of the Royals that now attend these private session "I expect that everyone has read this morning's paper how Peder Erikson has acquired an Iron ore mine in Northern Ontario and he has done so based on a very lucrative contract for himself and Aronia based on our demand for his Iron Ore. I think it is pretty apparent that the plan is coming together nicely."

"The question is being raised as how quickly he can have the mine producing high volumes of iron ore. Since we seem to be out of this recession, at least short term, demand has gone through the roof and the cries from our production facilities are coming in daily that the steel mills are falling way behind and the steel mills are screaming "where is our iron ore." Said Leif

"We need it fast King Dominique we are running ourselves ragged in the mines trying to pull out every ounce of ore as fast as we can to cover the short fall and late shipments of iron ore from abroad. It's causing shutdowns at factories that are blaming us." Mikkel told the King

"Hall said that from what Peder tells him and the information he received that there should be almost immediate results after the purchase of this mine." Mikkel added

"And so there would be but the government held up the purchase for a short time, the inspectors have to deem the mine safe. Peder said three weeks and they will be into full production." The King said

"The recession ending has put all the factories back in full production and the change to six hour shifts that we did to keep everyone in Aronia working is starting to cut into our production ability, believe it or not, being caused by a workforce shortage." Leif said with a bit of a laugh

"Shortage" the King exclaimed

"We are currently sending almost two hundred thousand of our working adults abroad each year your majesty which has caused a short term glitch in the ramp up speed in our production facilities. This has only been caused by the six hour work shifts instead of the eight hour shifts." Leif said "It will correct itself in a very short time but I just wanted to say it for a laugh and to show you we are really accomplishing something here."

"The emigration is moving very well and immigration is moving at an even slower rate. We are immigrating less than twelve hundred per year compared to, like Leif said, Two hundred Thousand emigrants per year not counting student Visas. It has been made clear to the students that they are expected to stay abroad and seek immigration at a later date and their task of promoting the Aronian way of life has had a national pride overtone that is ,well something I think should make us all very proud of our young people."

"The Increase is due in large part because of the economic upswing causing other countries the need for a well trained work force that their own countries can no longer supply and a reputation by our people as being highly efficient and productive workers. Canada as always has over fifty thousand a year emigrating from here Australia which was one of our concerns because of their stricter immigration policies have opened their doors a bit more freely in getting the man power they need as well." Erik announced

"The immigration by foreigners maybe down but we are status Quo on the student visa's I suggest we stay where we are at, in terms of amounts of students we allow in." said Eir

"The Odens Finger Development is completed and I am glad to say we have plenty of time now to develop other housing solutions thanks to our new emigration policies. Ivar announces

"Great, if that's it Mikkel why don't you stick around and we will see if we can get a hold of Peder and see if you can talk to Geir, maybe we can speed things up or send him some people to help. Perhaps you would like to go visit with Hall if you think it would help." The King purposed

The political red tape surrounding the mine was unchangeable the time lines and the procedures for safety where standard and Mikkel and Hall both understood why the government safety agency had done it, it was to protect the workers. The ore could be shipped almost immediately after that though but Peder had found a solution for the speed of getting the steel to the production facilities. He had an opportunity to buy a steel mill in Canada that was simply being given away.

The United States Steel producers had used the free trade agreement to block Canadian steel from crossing the border and had brought the Canadian steel companies to the edge of bankruptcy. The one mill, very close to the mine Peder had just purchased was the most efficient steel mill in the world and it was obtainable on the Toronto stock exchange at what Peter considered seven percent of what its true value was.

Mikkel pointed out that that would be taking jobs from Aronians in the Steel Industry. Peder said that the jobs would be going to Aronians just in another country and that Canada had been hit hard by the recession, Mikkel conceded noting that the Aronian steel mills could not keep up with the current demand and building another steel mill would take up much needed space.

Peder was given the thumbs up on buying the steel mill and the reopening of the mill and calling back all the steel workers and miners help to get the government safety agency to speed up the process and allow the mine to open in way less time.

Chapter XVI

Brian Finds Success but Never Peace

Brian's situation couldn't be better financially; he was a millionaire several times over with saferclip sales in the millions. Ontario wasn't the only place that decided that the Saferclips should be mandatory and the barge industry and the oil industry needed them to speed up production as well as safety. Brian had started his own tool company revolutionizing the concrete industry and every other antiquated industry he could find.

He hated working at Pre Fab Concrete Structures but without working there he may never have realized how backwards the industry was. He recalls working hoeing the concrete on his last day and he asked the guys he was working with "what's concrete made out of?"

The guys all started laughing thinking he was stupid and said "cement, gravel and water, there's a bunch of chemicals too." They said

Brian said "so Armageddon happens tomorrow, the hand full of survivors start building a new society and they need to find someone to make and build their infrastructure with concrete. Do you show up for the job? Brian asked

"Yah buddy ten years' experience" Carlos said

"Great we're so glad to have you come and save us, could you make us concrete." Brian said mimicking a distressed woman

"I sure can" said Carlos

"How?" asked Brian

"I mix cement, gravel and wa—…"Carlos is stopped mid-sentence

"–No you don't, first you have to make the cement powder." Brian said

"Oh" Carlos said with a dumbfounded look on his face "I think it's just crushed limestone and I think they heat it." Carlos said

"Close two more ingredients, anybody know?" Brian asked the ten guys working in the concrete.

"You have all worked here all your lives and not one of you even want to guess" Brian asked

"There are different kinds of cement" Dick said

"Yes there are. I don't care which one you name pick one" Brian laughed thinking you don't know any of them you moron so what difference does it make how many different blends there are.

"Clay people and a sulphate, probably gypsum, half the Roman Empire knew that clay burnt to ash, Calcium or limestone crushed to a powder gypsum or volcanic ash all heated too ash and ground to a powder makes cement. So, with the education system of three hundred A.D, the people back in ancient Rome where still smarter than any of you are today." Brian said .

That was Brian's last day at Pre Fab, which was the day after he had received his first royalty cheque for eighty thousand dollars. He did a lap of the yard in his new B.M.W waving at the guys and laughing. At the end of the rest of the guys shift they found hockey tickets and four cases of beer with a note that said *"because you don't know any better"*

Brian's life had changed though in the eight years, so had his surroundings. Gone were the shack that consumed his time, gone was Pre Fab Concrete Structures and the idiocracy that worked there. Bjorn had been as good as his word ,he had taken Brian's saferclip invention to a manufacturing company in Toronto to have it produced in an equal partnership plan were they patented the saferclip worldwide for him under his name with themselves as sponsors. Brian would receive Twenty percent of the gross profit margins on every Saferclip sold. Bjorn knew that the design was sound and he could see that the saferclip would save thousands of fingers and even some live. What he couldn't understand was how no one else in the manufacturing sector could see the value even though the safety agencies were saying that it could be law as soon as Brian could get it manufactured. All it took for Bjorn to find a manufacture was him saying he had the device at the Aronian church one Sunday. Several

Aronians had started manufacturing firms in Canada and they were looking for new product lines, safety equipment happened to be one of them. The factory was state of the art and was run and operated by mostly Aronian immigrates both here and in Nova Scotia. Brian didn't care about that even though he had mentioned that his beliefs were that a workforce should have to be a cross section of the committee it works from, at least it was being made in Canada. The relationship between Brian and Strongback tools was perfect, they manufactured, Brian developed new products and received twenty percent on what they made and they were making millions on the Saferclips and the clips that went on them.

Brian had bought a nice big house and had his daughter living with him. Now that he had become wealthy and successful all his women friends wanted relationships. Brian's daughter Paige always thought her dad should get in a solid relationship but Brian wouldn't have it, he would tell her "that as soon as the Canadian government makes fair laws that only allow people to leave the relationship with what they put in, then he would consider marriage."

The days at the Coffee Pub were more enjoyable now too, probably because of Brian's better attitude, but his militant streak towards big business and bad government hadn't subsided in the least. Jason would keep pointing out that he was going to have to shoot himself now because he was a part of big business.

"There is good big business and bad big business Jason, the day I become bad big business I will shoot myself to save someone else the trouble. The difference is I create something and I employ Canadians to build it." Brian said

"And what do other big businesses do that's any different than you." Jason asked

"Did you not hear I created something, these CEO's get voted in by a bunch of paper pushing buddies and rip off the people that have done the inventing and developing? They pay government officials off to get the country the way that best suits their big business mandates. Half the things that were illegal twenty years ago in the white collar industry are common business now, "Brian said

"Like what" Jason retorts

"Hydro," Brian said "Steph that works here fell behind on her hydro bill, so she is trying to catch up but every time they send her a bill they send her a blue sheet of arrears and charge her eighteen bucks for the arrears notice. So they charge her interest on what she owes and eighteen dollars for the notice and she was only ninety dollars behind on her hydro. That's two hundred and forty percent interests, twenty percent in one month, then they charge late fees and interest on that if you don't pay it."

"That's not right and they shouldn't do that. " Jason had to admit

"It's illegal or at least it used to be, its loan sharing and these city run corporations are doing it all the time as well as these phone companies. If I am working for you and I stop working do you pay me my wages for the next two years? If the phone company is screwing me and I take them back my phone because they suck, how do I owe them for two years of services when I'm no longer being served?" Brian said getting all fired up. "They can then hit my credit rating without taking me to court"

"Yah I remember the gas company got nailed for it years ago and had to pay back the money and I believe the charge was loan sharking. I don't know how they are getting away with it? "John said," but with the phone you sign a contract."

"They broke the contract by not giving the service they promised at the price they promised that's why you don't want their stinking phone, and the phones no good because it only works on their network. If I have to finish paying for the phone in that contract I could understand, but they make each phone so it only works for one company and I'm paying for hours of phone service I will never receive that's the one they can't justify." Brian's ranting was at full speed now

"Who's gonna do anything about it, they all pay the government and law enforcement to have them cater to their needs even though we are the ones paying the Government and the police their wages. That's the irony of it which is even worse; it's our money paying all these idiots to screw us. Think about it who are the police really protecting, we pay them huge buck to give us tickets for seatbelts and no insurance, oh guess the insurance companies got their money back on that lobbyist and when the citizens of this country finally decide to act like men and go after these thieves who do you think is getting the protection, yah, they have all of us paying for their protection if the bottom falls out of their scam."

"The Problem is Canadians won't stand up for or against anyone or anything, they need someone to tell them what to do, on everything and that's been caused by the people who are ripping them off. Take for example when Mulroney did the open floor vote on the death penalty. We know that the poll said that the vast majority of the country's population, seventy three percent according to the Gallup poll, supported the death penalty but when the vote went through the death penalty was defeated 148 to 127. Obviously the people we put in place to voice our opinions only voiced their own or whoever paid them's opinion, yet no one got shot for it. Any decent democratic citizen would have shot their representative for treason." Brian said ready to explode

"Why do you always have to end in shooting someone?" Jason laughed "We can't just vote them out?"

"And replace them with who" Brian asked "We have two parties, the bad party and the worse party, that both get money from the same capitalist pigs calling the shots. Why do you think bearing arms against oppressive governments is wrong, they call you a terrorist, they like that word it gets a lot of mileage?

"You don't just go around shooting people." Jason said as if it were just stupid.

Brian smiled and said* "Thomas Jefferson would disagree, he said [1]"No man shall ever be debarred the use of arms." "The strongest reason for the people to retain the right to keep and bear arms is, as a last resort, to protect themselves against tyranny in government." And he was part of the governing power at the time."

"If a man is getting beaten and doesn't put a stop to it does he A, like it, B deserve it or C been beaten for so long he doesn't even know it's wrong for them to be beating him." Brian asked like he's on a quiz show

"HONK! And awe times up the answer is C too stupid to even know it's wrong, they tell him it's his fault so he thinks he deserves it. B works as well I guess because if you don't fight back you do deserve it." If a Man goes Bankrupt society instantly says it's because he drank, smoked or managed his money foolishly. Strange thing is while he was doing well no one thought he was doing anything wrong but you never hear people saying 'poor fellow couldn't afford to live because his wage never increased to keep up with food, gas, hydro, and taxes'." as Brian answered his own question

Society was in fact getting even less knowledgeable and Brian was sure it wasn't going to change. His Daughter was extremely intelligent and she had done it without having everyone despise her, something that her father had too credit the fact that she may be more intelligent than him. He had taught her to read and love it at three, by eight she was reading five hundred page novels faster than he could. He taught her math and how to do it in her head, science and its relevance in everyday life and History. He also taught her sociology, people and the problems they cause and how they're being manipulated by media and warned her not to let that happen to her.

Brian learned early that he better take over the teaching part of his Daughters upbringing. When Paige was in grade two she had an assignment to mark and colour all the provinces and territories on the map of Canada and she asked dad to check her work, as always, and he asked "well aren't you supposed to mark Labrador on the map of Canada." Then he noticed the map had the ocean coast on the Quebec border. He got out an old atlas and had his daughter draw in Labrador and he wrote a letter to the teacher as though he was from Labrador telling the teacher that the people of Labrador believe Paige deserves extra credit for pulling them out of the ocean. The teacher told Brian when he saw her, months later, that she had never noticed and that they had used that map for years. Well there's one generation of children that will be taking their children to the beach in Quebec to see the ocean.

One day after school he was checking Paige's history and the paper said A.D. stood for

after death. He told Paige she had it wrong it
stands for anno domini which is Latin for "in the
year of the lord". Paige told him that she didn't
write that her history teacher did because Paige
had said it was Latin for in the year of the lord and
the teacher marked her wrong. Brian confronted
the history teacher and asked her where she had
heard that. She said that that is what it stood for,
she was taught it in University and it is part of the
curriculum and that Brian was wrong. Brian
simply asked her "If B.C stands for before Christ
and A.D stands for after death are the years while
Christ was alive known as T.M.Y the missing
years. Then he laughed at her. Paige asked her
dad to never talk to her teachers again.

Chapter XVII

Peder's Seeds of Success

Peder had watched the seeds of his people grow and expand without the need of him designating too much of his time or effort. Like business, Peder found that it was all about situating the right people in the right positions to help cultivate the society he was building. Though at first it seemed strange waking up and getting ready for church every Sunday it was one thing Peder and his family never missed. He was now a symbol to the Aronian people of their central roots and what could be accomplished by any Aronian. Many of the Aronians had started business' in Canada and were sponsoring and employing many Aronian immigrants which helped their business to succeed. The Aronians that were sent by the Royals and Aronian immigration would be tested and educated to specifically help that Aronian staff his business with the best.

The church, essentially an Aronian history class, was more a support group for fellow Aronians. If an Aronian needed anything they would just have to mention the fact at church and someone would help them out with whatever they required. The church was also a way for Aronians to show their social position and success. After only eight years many couples that had come to Canada as newlyweds where already needing full ten seat pews in church for their families. Not that the babies knew what the Great Book was yet the thousands of babies that would show up Sundays at Aronian churches were always the highlight of the day and as much a symbol of Aronian culture as Peder was. Every week hundreds of Canadian born Aronians were added to the Aronian citizenship in an honorary ceremony at the church, much like a Canadian baptism.

The church was also a tool Peder used in business take overs. When Peder was allowed to start buying the iron ore mine he was vested very largely in the sister high-rise condo to Erikson tower, office skyscraper and a subdivision. The housing was needed for all the new Aronians coming over. Real estate had been very profitable for Peder with all the Aronian engineers and skilled trades doing the work and a guaranteed sale to an Aronian as soon as it was built. So church also became a way for Peder to tap extra capital from Aronian investment. Church was the place where the Aronians were told when to buy, sell, and how to vote at shareholders meetings. With the Steel mill, the congregation was told to buy at anything under three dollars, sell at anything over five dollars then Peder would put a takeover bid in of four fifty and settle at five.

The mine was obtained for pennies compared to what Peder and the Royals had expected. The mine was scheduled to close soon because the vast quantities of ore remaining in the mine were of a very low grade. Aronia had been at this point with their mines a decade ago and had found many refining processes to make their iron ore as good as any. Geir could not believe that a country would close a mine with that amount of proven resources just because it was a poor grade and from the core samples Geir saw he was sure there was still some top grade ore in the area. The American block of Canadian steel under the free trade agreement made not only the mines very inexpensive but the steel mills as well.

The King did not like the idea Peder had to refine the ore and make the steel in Canada. He felt that was taking positions away from Aronian citizens. When Peder explained the recession had been very tough on Canada and by refining the iron ore in Canada and making the steel in Canada the shipping costs would be more economical and that there would be more jobs for Aronian immigrants. Peder explained that the political move of the U.S. in blocking the steel was an effort by the government to destabilize the Canadian steel industry, thereby making it possible for American corporations to take over the Canadian steel and mining companies using their overvalued currency. "In my opinion King Dominique they're doing it in the steel and lumber industry, this would be a good opportunity to look at that industry as well, lumber is always an issue in Aronia and they have almost bankrupted the companies over here". The King discussed Peder's views on the matter with his experts and they all agree with Peder. The minister of finance was afraid that the royal treasury could not afford such a grand endeavour but agreed that it may very well turn long term profits. The Royal Treasury had been stretched to the limit with the immigration departments' budget of baby bonuses, start-up funds for all the Aronians who were qualifying for immigration to Canada and the student tuitions of all the students going to Canada and abroad. He thanked Peder for the monetary contributions he had been making to the Aronian immigrants in Canada and told him it was defiantly helping. He felt that Peder's plan stood on solid grounds and felt that they should definitely do it but he would need some time to budget it.

When Peder got the message from the King, Peder told the King to tell Prince Rolf the acquisitions could be handled on this end and that he should lower the start-up money because Aronians here could help out, "they can all afford to do their part, they are making tens of thousands of dollars every-time we take over another company in the stock market." Peder told him.

The King gave Peder the green light. In ten years Peder had accomplished building the Aronian community in Canada; built corporations listed on the Toronto stock market and were now financing the Kings plan on its own merit. When the King would think back to the man that had come to the Royal palace twelve years ago, that wanted his ideas heard, the man that Dominique instantly liked, trusted, and believed in, the King had no idea that Peder could make his dream come true this fast! Peder and everyone helping him were accomplishing everything way beyond Dominique's expectations and Dominique was now sure that he would live to see his dream completed. Dominique was thankful that Peder and Margot were at the helm, Frid was a good man and was responsible for much of what Peder had accomplished but the King was worried about Frid's personal ego. Frid was all about money, power, and success. When King Dominique discussed this with Peder, Peder seemed to acknowledge and accept the problem said. "He is the best and he will accomplish our task faster and at a greater profit than any other could." Peder said to the King. "I will not let his ambition compromise our plan my King, of this you can be sure".

Chapter XVIII

King Reveals Success

At the morning breakfast with the Royals Vivian, Prince Erik and Lars would attend. "Morning everyone, as you have noticed three more chairs have been filled at our breakfast table this morning. Queen Vivian has joined us before and Prince Erik has attended from time to time but this is Lars first time" King Dominique said as the rest of the table clapped.

"Always a pleasure to see your face at our morning breakfast meeting Queen Vivian and welcome Prince Lars to your breakfast with the Royals. You may find us a bit much this early in the morning but please don't let that spoil your appetite". Val smiled and laughed reaching out and shaking the Royal Princes hands.

This will be a permanent arrangement for it is time for my boys to learn what will be required of them.

"Here here" shouted Val.

"here here" shouted the table.

'Now I don't want anyone to feel that I have brought them here as a shield, say your mind and say it true."

"Today I have the whole family here and I need all to hear and understand what I say, it is a very important day for all Aronia but none can know except who is in this room. That is why we have no servants today."

"I have in stealth to many of you, been deploying a plan to secure Aronia a stable secure future. I have deceived many in my ploy, an act I have not till this time ever had to do, but it is done and it has rewarded so many that the indignity of preforming this ruse was worthy of my sacrifice and the sacrifice of others integrity to the truth". Dominique's sister's face turned white, it was not the fear that her brother had done something horrible whether it be for the good of Aronia or not. It was shock by the fact the boy who had held her in confidence their whole lives had acted in something that Gertrud could tell was earth moving without confiding in her. The rest of the family that didn't know ,which were Vegar, Alex, and Julius sat with their mouths open and their eyes no longer blinking, the look of anticipation and bewilderment was almost identical in every face. No one even seemed to be breathing except for those who already knew and Queen Vivian.

"We all know that the natural resources of Aronia are slowly becoming either unobtainable or in short demand from our own mines". The statement so far had still pretty much left those not already in the know without reason to take a breath and seemed to make many even more anxious wondering if Aronia had run out of natural resources, so Vegar and Alex looked as though they were about to cry.

"One very smart and very dedicated Aronian stepped up and made the suggestion that will save our country. I sent Mr. Peder Erikson and his family on a mission to aid our country in a time of need, out of their home land, a place they loved, to do the impossible. He took sole responsibility for accomplishing my task and hundreds of thousands of Aronians joined to help him in his quest. Several hundreds of thousands have be sent on patriotic duties to other countries as well with my and Peder's dream in mind. But today Mr. Erikson has succeeded not only in what I had asked of him but much more. Mr. Erikson with the help of his family and eight hundred thousand Aronian nationals and students have obtained control of one of Canada's largest iron ore mines and one of the world's most efficient steel mills and processing facilities. He has also captured control of many of Canada's soft wood lumber mills and industries. He has done this in ten and a half years and secured Aronia a steady supply of natural resources for hundreds of years, maybe forever as long as success and Aronia are at his side.

Everyone at the table applauded and stood up to give the King a standing ovation. Queen Vivian's eyes looked up at Dominique as you would expect they looked up at him the day he first asked her out, her smile so proud that the Kings muscles tense up, his shoulders broaden and his chest expanded with an enormous breath of fresh air with the unmistakable taste of success.

"Peder Erikson", he continued, "Not only did more than I had asked he did it in a way that made Aronia and its people more accepted by Canada and the world, praised by all and loved by Aronians. 'The Great Book' has only three pages for national heroes left blank after King Domi put in every name of those who fought the conquistadors and died, two hundred have been added since then. I today nominate Peder Erikson to the ledger of national heroes and when he feels he can leave his duties, he and his family will be honoured at a banquet with those in this room attending to watch his name be entered, will you second?" Everyone's eyes were frozen to King Dominique as Val stands up,

"I'll…"

"No!" Gertrud reached over the table and grabbed Val pulling him down in his seat like only a big sister could. Dominique's eyes lit up and the blood ran to his face.

"I'll second that motion father" Prince Eric had stood up at the same time as Val but had refrained in respect not to interrupt his uncle Prince Val. Gerturd sitting beside the King was the only one that noticed and stopped Val to allow the next to the throne to make his first Royal act, a Royal decree that would be in the great book.

"Here here" cried Val.

Water filled Vivian's eyes "well done".

"Well done" cried Val and everyone at the table.

The King, who felt that this had been the best day of his life, was now enjoying the proudest day of his life as well. After thinking about it he succumbed to it being a mere second to the day he had wed Vivian and the day she had given him his first son.

"The motion carries" said the King.

Chapter XIX

Erikson's World

Peder Erikson was now the CEO of Canadian Resource Development Corp, Frid Gunder was his CFO, and Geir Sigurdur was president. The companies were severed so that the real estate company, Erikson Development corp. which Peder was CEO and where Peder put his best: architects, engineers, and accountants on the board. Both companies were doing well and their stock prices soared. The market loved acquisitions and both companies were making record numbers of them. They were now mining; copper, gold, silver nickel, diamonds and oil.They expanded internationally for lithium and aluminum, utilizing the Aronian immigrants in other countries. Peder had done it all. Peder Erikson's face was known by anyone who had ever picked up a business paper. Canadian business man of the year, Forbes top one hundred richest men year after year, he was given the key to more Canadian Cities than you could count. Everyone wanted to be him, everyone wanted to know him. When Peder Erikson shook your hand in front of a camera you knew you had an election in the bag. Peder and Margot had had twelve children, one hundred and fourty four grandchildren, which worked out to be about three birthday parties a week. For Peder there was no higher degree of social standing they could ever achieve. Not only was he successful enough to have twelve children but all twelve children were successful enough to have twelve children as well, but they would be the last generation to have that the honour of a that big of families, in Canada at least. Education would be used to keep what happened in Aronia fifty years ago from happening in Canada today and it would be the people's decision to do so.

Over the course of fifty years Peder had spread the population of Aronian Canadians across Canada, building high-rise condos and settlements in every Canadian city. He had churches, schools, and cultural centers in every city to accompany them. Every Aronian and every community was connected by media with Aronian television stations, radio stations everywhere and the internet. The Aronian culture was kept tight and supportive and no one strayed from their beliefs. There were Canadian born Aronians in many government seats for all three parties and at all three levels, provincial, federal and municipal. They ran charities and had minor league sports teams but even though they seemed to fit in with the rest of the Canadians they rarely connected socially and they never intermarried.

There were some that thought that the integration, or the lack of by the Aronians, was a plot or a conspiracy and there was even a newspaper that had started up denouncing any more immigration by Aronia or any other culture that would create a foreign entity greater than the original Canadian Identity and those who had built the country. The paper was shut down because it was deemed racist propaganda and then reappeared as a underground paper and radio show. Peder would tell the Aronians at church and through Aronian media that ' these people who speak such things are jealous of Aronian intellect, our strong work ethic and our superior culture and that is why they must keep building separate schools for their children'.

Chapter XX

Stubborn, Bull-Headed Old Fool

Brian was an old man now; he had figured out the problems for the whole world and Canada and made himself the unhappiest guy in the world for most of his life doing so. The saying that ignorance is bliss now made total sense to Brian. What good was knowing if you can't change the outcome because everyone has become too ignorant to understand what you're talking about when you tell them of the impending threat. What good is trying to educate the people when they have become too lazy and just don't want to put the effort forward to care?

Brian often thought what would have happened if the day he had figured out what was going on, what if he had of blown something up then or started shooting people by himself would someone else have followed would he have found someone else who cared. Brian had started a newspaper but no one ever bought it or read it or ever cared about what it said, it had cost him his friendship with Bjorn, a friendship Brian dearly missed. Bjorn understood Brian's reasoning but could not separate the rational from the personal. Brian understood Bjorn's point about the wrong people reading the paper and taking inappropriate actions and that it would drive a wedge between the two cultures, and Brian took his opinion to heart carefully writing each article as to make sure no radical would miss interpret his writings.

Throughout history there had been rebellion, how did they do it, how did Louis Riel get the people to care enough to fight, to die, for what he believed in? Brian couldn't even get Canadians out to vote.

The people that Brian had hated most had surely lost the battle and he was glad of that and a much better man had won, but it still meant Brian had lost. The Country would probably be a better place; it would be more like what Brian had envisioned a perfect Canada to be,; only no real Canadians would be left in it, after the election was over. That would be the part Brian would not stand for.

Brian had made hundreds of millions by started his own tool company Industry Proven Tools. He designed some of the most innovative tools in the field and made every hard working Canadians life a whole lot easier. He opened factories and hired only third generation Canadians. He set up ventilation systems so if the guys wanted to smoke, they could and they kept the door locked so in his words " no one could do a damn thing about it." The men's locker room had pin up girls on the wall and god knows what was on the walls in the girl's locker room, if anyone was offended they could change in the bathroom or get another job. He made sure every worker had safe transportation to and from work by giving every man a Canadian made company car so insurance companies couldn't rip them off and Industry Proven could deduct; it, the car and the Hydro that ran them. Uniforms and boots where supplied and a hot lunch all deductible costing the company little saving the men lots. By doing this Brian also guaranteed that everything that was bought was made by a Canadian in Canada and he could have some pull with the large orders he made to make sure the rest of their products were made in Canada as well.

Brian believed in fighting back and he believed in winning. Brian's employees were given a per child bonus every Christmas and on the child's birthday, Brian's only wish was that more would have followed his cause. Brian's employees would do anything for Brian even though most still believed he was a crazy old man. He would stand outside of foreign owned steel mills and lumber operations caring pickets saying take back what is ours nationalize what's been stolen and the guys loved him so much they would march with him not really knowing what they were marching for even though Brian had tried to explain. Brian's son's from two other relationships would lead the rallies and help the old man hand out the educational material to inform everyone why the protests were happening.

He'd been locked up more than once by police and sent for mental evaluations more times than you could shake a stick at. Paige knew her Dad wasn't crazy he was just too smart for his own good which caused him to over react over things. She also knew that he wasn't really over reacting; he was just surrounded by a world of people who weren't reacting at all, so her Dad would try to be loud enough for everyone because he considered them too stupid to know they were being taken advantage of. Paige understood that people had reached the intellectual point of not caring because they couldn't understand and she knew that they had been programmed to feel that they couldn't do anything about it anyway. Unlike her father she felt sorry for them and their ignorance and didn't blame them for it.

Paige was her father's daughter, she was intellectually advanced and was able to deduce from the facts that revealed themselves. She did not feel the passion that her father did about revenge or justice but she understood that injustices were being done and, because there wasn't anyone else like her crazy dad, they would never be stopped. She was a surgeon for most of her life and she had never had to suffer for anything, her Dad did that for her so she would never have to go without and she wouldn't ever have to feel his bitterness.

Tonight Paige, now fourty five, goes to her fathers with Jenny her youngest of five because she knows her Dad better than anyone. Its election night and the old man had talked about tonight for fourty years. She knew he was going to do it, she knew she couldn't stop him, but she had to try and she had to see her Dad one last time.

"Dad I know what you're up to, here's

your Will back, like they would accept it in a court of law anyway. Being of sound mind, my ass. Dad, it has happened how many thousand times throughout history, please it will make your grandchildren's life hell." Paige begged her dad.

"It'll be the first time in my life I'll have done exactly what I want to do and exactly what every honourable man in this country should be doing. "Brian coughed as he tried to laugh "who knows with my luck I'll be second in line so I won't get to have any of the glory before I die."

Brian looked at Paige and said* "The tree of liberty, my dear Paige, must be refreshed from time to time with the blood of patriots and tyrants. It is its natural manure."
"Thomas Jefferson wrote that to William Smith. Don't act like you're so poetic and that's manure, you said it yourself they will run the country better and they will eventually beat the Oligarchy because, they are, what we should have been. Come on Dad." Paige pleaded

"It has nothing to do with what I like; it has to do with taking what isn't yours to take. Yes I believe in survival of the fittest but that needs an equal playing field and a set of rules as well. What I shall do tonight makes the rules a little more clear for generations to come," Brian said.

"I'll go with you then it's my duty too, hold on I'll just go tell your granddaughter what I'm doing, she's smart too, maybe she'll want to come along" Paige said to her Dad trying to show him what an ass he's being but knowing she had no chance of winning this fight.

"Don't be an ass; let an old man die in peace. I always told you that I would pick my own time and that I wasn't leaving it up to some celestial moron with a beard." Brian starts laughing then choking and coughing.

"That's from smoking you genius thought you were smart but you weren't smart enough to quit." Paige said just egging the old man on.

"You are the only love and happiness I've ever know Paige, mostly my own fault, so why are you here pissing me off now when I'm finally going to get to do what every honourable man should want to do and go out with a bang!" The old man said with a snarly old grin.

"Whatever you do Dad I'm glad and proud to have been so lucky to have a crazy old bird like you as my dad. I love you more than anything and I'll miss you so bad. Who am I going to talk to if you're not here," tears building in her eyes as she started to cry.

"Your kids, just like I did, teach them, protect them, tell the reasons and explain to them the facts of what happened. Make them draw their own conclusions don't do it for them. Let them chose whether their grandfather or great grandfather was a nutbar or a patriot. Paige write down everything I've ever said or done because history cannot forget. Plato warned us let me warn others. Now let me see my granddaughter, she hasn't figured out what I'm doing has she? Did you both vote?" Brian snapped

"Yes Dad everyone voted and no, but Jenny probably expects it" Paige said tears run down her face but she smiled and took in the image of her father the man that wouldn't yield

"Good, haha, funny if they didn't win huh." Brian laughed "It would be a good thing to be wrong once"

"No Dad you're never wrong you just go about solving things in a unique way" Paige said snuffling up the tears "Tomorrow I will be the daughter of a national hero and I'll make sure history is written that way."

"Don't be so damn melodramatic; never thought I'd be saying that to someone else. What I am doing is teaching, that is all and with any luck getting you and this country a bargaining chip so you can provide a stable environment for my grandchildren to live in this Country as equals. Your half-brothers have their orders, you lead them, guide them, you are the wisest, they have my passion." Brian said "Now let me say hello to that granddaughter of mine, then I think you better go." Brian said

They hug like they never want to let go of each other, Brian's eyes fill with tears, she would be the only thing he missed from this world the only thing that ever brought him joy.

"I Love you Paige, never change for anybody baby. Now hurry up I got to go soon, timings everything you know." Brian said not wanting to lose his resolve or Paige to see him crying.

Chapter XXI

Election 2040

Limits would now be set after the upcoming election and new immigration policies so what had happened in Aronia fifty years ago couldn't happen here in Canada and what happened in Canada fifty years ago couldn't happen in Canada again. It was election night and Peder's son Nikkulai was about to be elected Prime Minister of Canada. There was no chance of defeat he would win with the largest majority government in Canadian history the proudest day in Peder's life and King Dominique's, who would be gathering at the Erikson mansion tonight for the celebration.

King Dominique and Queen Vivian were greeted at Toronto's Pearson International Airport by hundreds of thousands of Aronians. The Aronian immigrants that originally came to Canada were told at church and at the community centers to stand on the edge of the street lining up side by side all the way to Peder Erikson's mansion their grandchildren behind them their children behind them. This way the smaller children would be able to see their King. King Dominique had asked for it to be this way because he wanted to be able to thank those first million that he had spoken of but could not fit them all into the Great Book. Seven million Canadian Aronians waving Aronian flags lined the streets of Toronto from the airport all the way to Peder's estate. The King thanked them all tears rolled down his cheeks as children ran out to give Queen Vivian roses, trilliums, and Aronian flags. Television cameras sent out live satellite digital pictures to every Aronatronic television across Canada so the millions of Aronians across Canada could watch.

The guards at the door of the Erikson estate didn't ask to see the King and Queens invitation but instead bowed to them as they drove through the gate. The Guards were wearing traditional uniforms of dark grey with golden buttons running up the front and elaborate gold rope embroidering on the sleeves. Their shoulders were covered in shiny armour shoulder pads and an armoured chest plate and neck plate of glimmering steel. Around their mid-section large pantaloons of gold and purple with a fur skirt inlayed with steel diamond shaped armour. They wore knee high leather boots with steel toes and steel bars running down the sides. On their heads they wore bright silver metallic curved helmets with large feathers from exotic birds on the side. The uniforms were fashioned after that of the conquistadors with a few Aronian changes. The yard was large with a long curved driveway as the topless limo passed the trees that obstructed the King and Queens view they could see the huge four story mansion. It was all made of giant limestone blocks with a slate roof with decorative green and red slate diamonds between the dormers, iron trimmings decorated the house everywhere with Ivey growing up the walls and gardens all over the grounds.

Peder and Margot couldn't wait inside to see them and there they stood with the front door open behind them looking warm and inviting to the King and Queen whose bodies were not used to Canadian temperatures.

The King did not wait for the guard to open the door for them; King Dominique opened the door and jumped out before the car had even stopped. "We did it, we did it!" the old man hollered at Peder.

"In the name of the King" Margot replied as she stepped down to the car to welcome the Queen to their home, leaving Dominique and Peder in a manly embrace.

"Old fools" the Queen said as Margot helped her out of the limousine. "How are you doing Margot, all of this excitement getting to you yet?"

"I've got to admit Queen Vivian seeing King Dominique and Peder this giddy, I'd swear they had just came out of the billiard room and planned this last week".

"I told you he wasn't going to be a spy, remember you were scared" laughed the Queen then she started coughing.

"Are you alright Queen Vivian?"

"Yes just get me out of the cold, I'm getting too old" she said as they walked past the men still hugging and punching each other playfully in the shoulders.

The Queen now walked with a cane her body more frail than Margot's, she was eighty now, her beautiful blonde hair that once ran passed her thigh was now white. She still had the elegance of royalty but her beautiful blue eyes were almost grey and her skin, once so soft and beautiful was wrinkled, worn and translucent.

"You asked me fifty years ago if I thought 'The King had chosen wisely by choosing Peder' and you asked me to answer honestly." Margot said

"I remember it like it was yesterday Margot. You were pregnant with Dominique full term, we were afraid you may give birth with the excitement" The Queen laughed with a small cough, "You wouldn't happen to have a small glass of brandy around here would you?"

"I just happen to and this time I can join you, I'm not pregnant, I don't think" Margot said with a grin

The Queen laughed "You said Peder had never failed at anything he had set out to accomplish. Boy were you right"

"I wasn't honest though, I wasn't sure then" Margot admitted.

They walked into the Parlour and Margot poured them both a warm brandy. "I saw Peder change that day into the most focused man I'd ever seen. When we arrived in Canada his drive and determination was unexplainable. You could see it in his eyes, he knew he would succeed and nothing of this world could stop him. I'm sure that is why he has lived this long and stayed so vibrant."

"Peder and Dominique can share the same pair of shoes Margot; they may be the only two men with the guts and determination to pull off what they've done. Great challenges make great men and today our husbands make world history; if they had been younger when they started they may have out done Alexander the great, but believe me their name will go down in history with Alexander. World history Margot, not just Aronian".

"Yes but they will be loved forever in Aronia, the rest of the world may not be so kind" Margot said with a bit of hesitation.

"The world respects greatness and you must write it just the way it happened. We are old but it must be written, I have already written what I know and I brought it for you to finish. I suggest you leave out them acting like two giddy school boys on your front porch."

"It's their moment, they have waited fifty two years to reap the fruit from the seeds they've planted, let them enjoy it." Margot said as she refills their glasses.

"So what happens after this?" Margot asked.

"Dominique will be crowning Erik King when we return. He's a good man just like Peder and his father but he said his son will make a better King than he, so he plans on doing a short rain and hopes Dominique and I get to watch our grandson get crowned. Dominique blames himself for keeping the crown so long, but he wanted to see this through."

"I'm sorry" Margot apologized, "We would have won the election four years ago but Peder wasn't sure about getting the Newfoundland vote or the Nunavut vote so he waited till he moved some more people there"

"I don't think four years would have made a difference dear Erik and his brothers and sisters have sat with their father on the Aronian Boards and done their parts, they are happy. Erik doesn't want his son to have to deal with the back lash of this little affair and he has prepared his whole life to handle what happens next. " Vivian smiled.

"Queen Vivian" Margot said looking at the door.

"You know I've always loved being called that, but for just one night call me Vivian or I'm going to call you Queen Margot".

"Oh my que… I mean Vivian." Margot bursted out.

"Vivian, should we not get those two fools off the porch?"

"They're still out there! God yes let's get them" said the Queen

"Knew you could do it Peder from the first time I laid eyes on you I was twenty eight-years old then you were thirty two, I believe." The King said remembering back

"For King and my country my King"

Peder laughed.

"My plan," said the King

"Whoa, who's plan?" Peder said

"My Plan!" Said the King standing up straight

Even at eighty years of age King Dominique was still an enormous, fit man but now his broad face was filled with wrinkles. His blue eyes still twinkled but his long blonde hair was now all grey.

"You wouldn't have had a plan if you hadn't seen my plan first," said Peder much smaller but still a fit man his blonde hair now all but gone but the same twinkle in his bright blue eyes as the Kings.

"Yours was just a suggestion that you gave the board."

"Okay true, but without it…"

"Oh yes Peder, You were my inspiration, my champion, and my 'conqueror'."

"What do you think King Domi would say if he was here?"

"Damn hadn't thought of that, probably something like 'Never let the fruits of your diligence spoil, reap the rites from the seeds you have sown and ensure the seed of tomorrow'."

"King Dominique, I think I have a tear" Peder laughed, "That is, what he'd say, damn poetic, we should write that down somewhere."

"Yeah, I just came up with it, we should give it to your son, Nikkulai and he can use it in his speech tonight."

"Yeah I'll text it to him, its good." laughed Peder. "So how's Queen Vivian?"

"She is so happy to see Margot again. She's probably going to ask you two to come join us in Aronia," the King said.

"Of course," said Peder

"For good if you like Peder, your job here is done if you and Margot would like to come home. We would like you to move into the palace with us, and you would be welcomed there for the rest of your days, at our age we shouldn't be in the cold." The King told Peder sincerely.

Peder hesitated "Spending time with you and Queen Vivian would be an honour and Margot is so happy when she's with her but all of our children are here."

"Well I know the Queen wants it but it is totally up to you. You do realize tomorrow morning your name goes down in history, you'll be a national hero in Aronia but it may be a bit dangerous for you here. Cats out of the bag as you put it."

"We'll be fine; the Oligarchy have trained all the fight out of these people. I'll have to ask Margot but I wouldn't mind the best of both worlds." Peder answered the King.

"Done, I always knew you were a smart cookie," joked the King.

"Come on in you two, it's freezing!" Margot yelled out the door.

"How are you my love? The Queen's missed you so much you look radiant." The King turned to Peder and gives him a wink as he hugs Margot.

"Don't you worry about us Margot, I've brought two bottles of Aronian scotch to warm us up and celebrate our victory." The King pulled two bottles out of his thick winter coat as Peder laughed wearing a button up shirt and just now noticing the thick winter coat the King had been wearing in September.

"Margot, doesn't Nikkulai want you and Peder to be there when he wins?" Queen Vivian inquired.

Margot laughed "We are here, he's with his family next door, Peder and I will go over and congratulate him when he wins. Then he will come over here where he can meet the King and you and pledge his allegiance to the crown of Aronia."

Margot and the Queen sat watching the television broadcast of the election results as Dominique and Peder talked about how Peder had divided the population of Aronians up around the country to the different electoral ridings before the election to guaranty every seat.

"Here it comes!" Margot screamed. Everyone was watching as the results came in on the giant screen television.

"Wow Lars it looks like it's going to be a landslide victory for the New Dominion Party. In the Maritimes with every seat in Newfoundland, Labrador, Prince Edward Island, Nova Scotia, and New Brunswick!"

"That's right Lisbet and we can't confirm yet but Quebec and Ontario No- Yes- Yes we can confirm about 80% of the polls are in and it's the same story in Quebec and Ontario looks to be the same! It's defiantly a majority government, the only thing that we're waiting for tonight is if the New Dominion Party takes every seat. But Nikkulai Erikson is defiantly Canada's new Prime Minister; let's take you there now to see his reaction".

"Shall we go my dear the world awaits our appearance?"

"We shall" Margot smiled at the King and Queen, "Que- sorry, Vivian we'll be right back."

Peder gave Margot a look of horror and shock. "She asked me to call her Vivian, what's the matter? Dominique still making you use your Majesty?" Margot laughed at Peder all the way to Nikkulai's house.

After Peder congratulated his son Margot gave Nikkulai a kiss. Peder kissed Hilda, Nikkulai's wife on the cheek and gave her a hug, and then he kisses all his great grandchildren and shakes the grandchildren's hands. Peder leans over Nikkulai's shoulder and tells his son "whenever you're ready".

Nikkulai entered his father's house the new elected leader of Canada in front of him stood King Dominique Olafur IV and Queen Vivian. Margot stood beside the Queen, Peder beside the King as

Nikkulai walked up and bowed to the King

"There is no need to bow to the King of Aronia Nikkulai, Aronians are all equal, we just have different functions to perform."

"Sorry your Majesty." Nikkulai said standing, "I Nikkulai Erikson pledge my allegiance to my King and the people of Aronia…

An old man steps out of a Canadian made electric Zinn car and walks up to the guards dressed in Aronian ceremonial uniforms.

"Excuse me I am Prince Val I am here to see my brother King Dominique and Peder Erikson." said the old man

"Prince Val I am honoured I will buzz the house and tell them that you are here." The guard said

Two silenced shots barely detectable whistle through the air dropping the two young guards dead in their tracks

"Hee hee good shot John not bad for your first kill" Brian said cackling with delight

"First kill my ass like you ever shot anybody before." John said walking around the edge of the bushes a sniper rifle in his hands

"I never said I did, but it feels good when you know it's the right thing to do, never thought that. I thought I'd still feel bad or something, not so much." Brian shrugged

Brian had planned on having to shoot the guards; he had hoped that the guards might open the gate without phoning the house, since Brian knew Prince Val was in Australia with Dominique's son Fjalar, that way he wouldn't have had to shoot them. But Brian realized Aronians even Canadian born Aronians were to efficient to not follow protocol, he was happy that the guards didn't know what Val looked like or his whereabouts.

"Gotta go give our new King a big hug and wish our new Prime minister a safe journey to hell." Brian said as he opens his trench coat exposing layers of explosives giggling. His bald head and age spots, covered by his fedora, and with the high collar of his trench coat flipped up, all you could see were his bright blue eyes shining beneath his hat. The disguise and the way he pranced around would make you think that a much younger man was concealed beneath the cloak.

See you on the other side in a few years John you've been a good dear friend. Oh leave the gloves in the car we don't want you getting busted and going away for life" Brian chuckled

"Don't you have too much fun or you'll die before you get to the house you crazy old man. See you in a few years at the coffee shop in the sky so we can debate for eternity, good friend. If you don't get them all I promise I'll give it my best." John said solemnly

"Well there are about fifty million of them for you to take target practice on, once I'm gone" Brian yelled after him "Would make it hard to miss" he muttered to himself

A black limousine pulled up to the entrance way before the gate to pick John up. Jason stepped out of the driver's door and looked over the hood of the car.

"You had to shoot them?" He said only slightly shocked "Good luck Brian I hate to admit it, you were right, I'll miss arguing with you and I'll tell my grandchildren everything that happened here tonight so history remembers.

Good bye old friend." Jason said as he drove away with John in the back.

"Goodbye old friends" Brian said remembering all the good time the three of them had shared.

Brian liked the Aronians he liked their beliefs he liked their advanced knowledge, their efficient nature. There was no hate here it was just a matter of pride, of honour ,in Brian's mind there was no way he was going to allow some country to take over his country with no casualties, no fight. History has to show that at least one Canadian fought to keep what his forefathers worked so hard to build hopefully it would show three good friends fought together.

Brian walks up to the gate with one of his tools and simply cuts the hinges off, got into his electric Zinn loaded with explosives and whistling Oh Canada, drove down the long curved lane thinking, I don't want to hurt these beautiful old Oak Trees they're very nice."

Nikkulai kissed his parents and shook the Kings hand as they said there farewells and congratulations. Peder walked up to Nikkulai and whispers how proud he was of his son as Nikkulai got in the limousine with his wife. The children and grandchildren climbed into Aronibus vans to follow the procession to the New Dominion Party Headquarters and the victory celebration.

"Good evening Mr. Prime Minister we will be heading to the Campaign hall as soon as the R.C.M.P arrive, shall we meet them at the gate." The chauffeur asked

    "Yes if we must wait, drive to the road."
Nikkulai said a little perturbed
    "The R.C.M.P wasn't ready for such an
early result" said the driver

Chapter XXII

The Exodus

The next day Canadian airports would have been flooded with millions of Aronians flying into the country, the jets, the paper work and the people from Aronia, most with military training, had already been readied. By years end immigration laws into Canada would have been changed as well. Anyone without full Canadian citizenship would be deported unless they were Aronian, all prisoners who had citizenship somewhere else would be sent back from where they came. Many would try and leave, and The Aronian Canadian government would let them, the French and the Native Canadians would probably chose to fight. Some may stay but would receive low positions that would only allow for one child per couple that would end in extinction in a century or so. Many Canadians of non-Aronian descent would want to immigrate to other countries, many would want refugee status. Australia would take in three hundred thousand Canadian refugees; imagine their shock when they would find out that their refugees were Aronian Canadian refugees, but we can't discriminate that would be politically incorrect.

The plan was set; Democracies across the globe would fall.

"Told you it would work." Peder would say.

The King would laugh, "How did you know that Australia would take that many refugees?"

"Because democracy has to show they protect their own, we already had enough to form a minority government there. So in twenty years as soon as the next generation can vote, who'd of thought of using Democracy as a weapon?" Peder would laugh   "We did". They would say together

That's the way it could have been, that's the way it would have been if the world was a politically correct place and everyone was a politically correct little robot. But Brian believed in rebellion he believed that the only way to stop injustice was to stomp it out. His daughter had grown into a strong intelligent woman and could take care of herself now and Brian could be himself. Brian felt that Canadians were getting what they deserved by being so naïve but he couldn't let history show that every Canadian was stupid and spineless.

The R.C.M.P. had been dispatched to the Erikson estate to escort the next Prime Minister of Canada to the New Dominion Party campaign hall. Most of the men were stunned at the election results some had even voted for them but now they were frightfully aware of what had just happened some just didn't understand. The Canadian Aronian R.C.M.P officers were ecstatic over the results.

As the cruisers pulled up to the intersection leading to the estate, a Limonene pulled up to them flagging them down.

"Where the hell have you been!" shouted the driver," We should have been at the New Dominion headquarters ten minutes ago, the results have been in for half an hour." The driver screamed

The cruisers wheel around and the constable told the limo driver to follow them. The procession speeds down the streets heading to the giant conference hall that is the New Dominion Party headquarters, then, at the last corner leading up to the hall the limo sped away going straight through the intersection.

"Where the hell is he going" the Sergeant said to the Constable

"Don't know" the Constable shrugged "But the old bastards flying" he said

"Radio it in "the Sergeant said as he wheeled the cruiser around in pursuit.

The limousine drove into an Industry Proven warehouse on the docks of Toronto, the doors closed behind them. The R.C.M.P Radioed into headquarters that they are afraid the new Prime Minister may have been kidnapped send all vehicles to the waterfront for backup.

John and Jason got out of the limousine laughing "sad isn't it that they were dumb enough to fall for that" Jason said climbing into the speed boat.

'Isn't that the problem our friend is about to die for?" John said the sad reality setting in

"It's how he wanted to go, anything else would not have been melodramatic enough for him. Think it's done?"

"I would have thought we'd hear the blast even from here." John said

"Exciting, fooling the cops and the car chase, who would of believed a bunch of old buggers like us could have this much fun at this age." Jason said speeding out onto Lake Ontario

Brian drove down the lane of the Erikson Estate thinking to himself "Will they write about me like Che Guevara or like the Palestinians, or the Al Qaeda. If the Aronians are in charge it will definitely be the Al Qaeda for sure, if it's the Oligarchy it will be the Palestinians, they wouldn't want to make anyone that does something like this, out as an act of heroism. If my daughter and mankind win, fat chance, I will be written of like Che but hopefully they write about Paige as Che with a better outcome."

Brian's thoughts stop as a big smile grew on his face "for liberty, justice and Thomas Jefferson he yells as he speeds up and meets the Prime ministers limousine around the corner of the big oak trees.

Prime Minister Marcel St. Pierre had been shown as leading the polls but had heard word that the Aronians wouldn't answer pollsters. As the first results had come in from the Maritimes he knew instantly what had happened and was ashamed of how his name would go down in History as the fool who lost Canada to a foreign country without so much as a fight. The Canadians that had suspected foul play had been tagged as conspiracy theorists, nutbars and racists.

Prime Minister St. Pierre had locked himself in his office and was thinking "What can I do to save face, to not go down in history as an idiot." when he heard the news.

"Mr. Prime Minister Mr. Prime Minister, Nikkulai Erikson has just been killed; he and his family have been murdered by a man driving a car bomb." Screamed the Prime Ministers assistant Chad

The Prime Minister thought he was dreaming "could it be he had a second chance to fix this". He ran out of his office screaming orders, his path was obvious.

"Call the senate, I'm imposing Martial law this instance and do not use the word murder about the man who just saved your ass," said the Prime Minister. "And use the term freedom cell as the 'people' responsible to the press, and Chad get everyone of Aronian descent out of this office immediately.

In London City an old man sits in his antique high back leather chair behind the most intricate beautiful antique desk from the 17th century. Behind him a eight foot tall painting of a hooked nosed man leaning against a pillar in the old London stock exchange. The results of the Canadian election were inevitable but he had stayed up to watch, just to be thorough.

He knew this would be a problem, but the family had insisted that he let it play out and see if they could obtain a foot hold in Aronia. He had known that as long as Dominique refused child rearing ages to migrate to Aronia they would never get a foot hold in Aronia , they had been trying since the eighteenth century, but now he had a real problem.

He calls to his secretary "Set up a conference call of the Bilderberg directing members, for after the gold fixing."

THE END

Thomas Jefferson Quotes

"…wherever the people are well informed they can be trusted with their own government; that whenever things get so far wrong as to attract their notice, they may be relied on to set them to rights."

-Thomas Jefferson
Letter to Richard Price 1789

"The strongest reason for the people to retain the right to keep and bear arms is, as a last resort, to protect themselves against tyranny in government."

-Thomas Jefferson

"No free man shall ever be debarred the use of arms (with in his own lands).

-Thomas Jefferson
Purposed Virginia constitution June 1776

"The tree of liberty must be refreshed from time to time with the blood of patriots and tyrants. It is its natural manure."

-Thomas Jefferson
Letter to William Smith November 3. 1787

About the Author

Leslie Bruce Irwin was born in Woodstock, Ontario Canada and lives in London Ontario. He is an Inventor, Designer by trade with industrial safety equipment in the construction field and award winning costume designs for theatrical presentations. He has spent most of his life working in the construction field and was very active in municipal government, election campaigns and sitting on boards and committees.

Leslie's passion for literature was more of an obsession with reading more than writing, for most of his life. Mr. Irwin considers the written word sacred and the best way to quench the thirst for knowledge. He is self-taught in economics, political science and philosophy and attended Fanshawe college for Industrial design.

Leslie's passion for writing occurred later in life when material on subjects that he considered important didn't exist. He felt that the void must be filled with material that would challenge the intellect at different levels and be something that everyone could read, learn while enjoying the story. Fiction writers such as Ayn Rand, George Orwell, Joseph Heller and Ray Bradbury would be considered strong influences in his story genre and writers such as Anne Rice and Dan Brown would be influences on his writing style.

Mr. Irwin uses fiction to make people aware of real problems and social injustices that he believes are occurring in today's society. He writes in the hope that others can make their own connections and perhaps do their own research to someday build a better world.

If you had only one word in the English language to describe another human being you would have to choose "Dreamer" for Mr. Irwin even though he prefers the term Idealist.

Reference material

**Fear of Crime and Attitudes to Criminal
Justice in Canada: A Review of Recent Trends
2001-02**
Julian V. Roberts
Department of Criminology
University of Ottawa
Fear of Crime and Attitudes to
Criminal Justice in Canada:
A Review of Recent Trends[1]
2001 - 02
The percentage of the public endorsing capital
punishment has fallen to a historic low of 52%,
down from 73% in 1987.
© Amnesty International Canada 2011
A motion to reintroduce capital punishment was
debated in the House of Commons in 1987. On

June 30, the motion was soundly defeated on a free vote (148-127), despite public opinion polls indicating majority support for the death penalty.

Religion: A Bold Stand on Birth Control
By Roberto Suro: Richard N Oatling :Michael P Harris Monday, Dec. 03, 1984

Read more:
http://www.time/time/magazine/article/0.9171923 776.00.html#ixzz1aLehLFZF

World Oligarchy

In 2001, Denis Healey, a Bilderberg group founder and, for 30 years, a steering committee member, said: "To say we were striving for a one-world government is exaggerated, but not wholly unfair. Those of us in Bilderberg felt we couldn't go on forever fighting one another for nothing and killing people and rendering millions homeless. So we felt that a single community throughout the world would be a good thing."
^ Ronson, Jon (10 March 2001), "Who pulls the strings? (Part 3)" (The *Guardian* (London). http:www.guardian.co.uk/books/2001/mar/10/extr act1. Retrieved 14 May 2009.
Sensing its ability to foster international cooperation, a number of prominent thinkers and politicians on the far left and far right have criticized the Trilateral Commission. On the right, in his book *With No Apologies,* former

conservative Republican Senator Barry Goldwater lambasted the discussion group by suggesting it was "a skillful, coordinated effort to seize control and consolidate the four centers of power: political, monetary, intellectual, and ecclesiastical...[in] the creation of a worldwide economic power superior to the political governments of the nation-states involved."\l Goldwater, Barry; coauthored with Stephen Shadegg (1980). *With No Apologies*. Berkley. p. 299.

Is It Possible

All data from Migration Policy Institute

Comparing Migrant Stock: The Foreign Born in Australia, Canada, and the United States by Region of Origin
Australia, Canada, and the United States are all considered "traditional countries of immigration." All three countries also categorize their immigrants by place of birth, providing an opportunity to compare some aspects of their foreign-born populations. These graphs provide a window on the origins of immigrants in each of these countries to help explain the immigration patterns that give rise to unique immigrant populations.

Australia

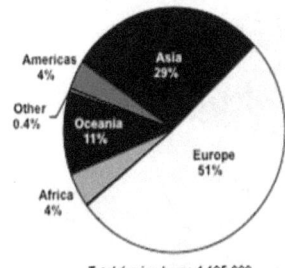

Region of Birth for the Foreign-Born Population of Australia, 2001

Americas 4%
Asia 29%
Other 0.4%
Oceania 11%
Europe 51%
Africa 4%

Total foreign born: 4,105,688

•   There were 4.1 million foreign born in Australia in 2001, representing 22 percent of the total population of 19.0 million.

•   Over half of all immigrants in Australia are from Europe, predominantly the United Kingdom, but Italy, Greece, Germany, and the Netherlands are also among the largest source countries.

•   Almost one-third of all immigrants in Australia are from Asia. Vietnam, China, the Philippines, and India are among the largest source countries.

•   Compared with Canada and the United States, Australia has the highest percentage of immigrants from Oceania, mostly from New Zealand.

Canada

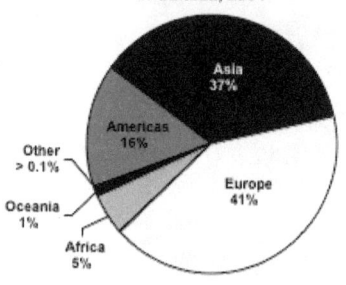

Region of Birth for the Foreign-Born Population of Canada, 2001

Total foreign born: 5,647,125

- There were 5.6 million foreign born in Canada in 2001, representing 19 percent of the total population of 30.0 million.
- The majority (41 percent) of all immigrants in Canada are from Europe. The United Kingdom, Italy, Poland, Germany, and Portugal are among the largest source countries.
- Over one-third of all immigrants in Canada are from Asia. China, India, Hong Kong, and the Philippines are among the largest source countries.
- Compared with Australia and the United States, Canada has the highest percentage of immigrants from Africa, including South Africa, Egypt, and Morocco.

United States

Region of Birth for the Foreign-Born Population of the United States, 2000

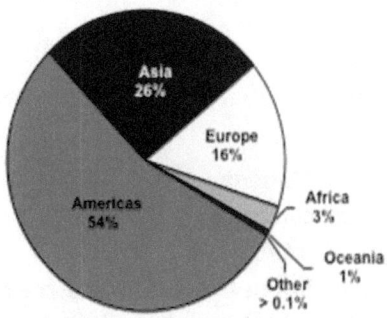

Total foreign born: 31,107,889

There were 31.1 million foreign born in the United States in 2000, representing 11 percent of the total population of 281.4 million.

• Over half of all immigrants in the United States are from the Americas, predominantly Mexico, but Cuba, Canada, and El Salvador are also among the largest source countries.

• Over one-fourth of all immigrants in the United States are from Asia. The Philippines, India, China, Vietnam, and Korea are among the largest source countries.

• Only 16 percent of all immigrants in the United States are from Europe. Germany is one of the largest source countries.

Statistics Canada

www.statcan.gc.ca

Page content follows

Immigration in Canada: A Portrait of the Foreign-born Population, 2006 Census: Portraits of major metropolitan centres

Toronto: Canada's major immigrant gateway

The census metropolitan area (CMA) of Toronto is still the major gateway for immigrants in Canada.

The census enumerated 2,320,200 foreign-born people in Toronto in 2006, the largest number of any metropolitan area in the nation. Between 2001 and 2006, the foreign-born population grew by 14.1%, compared to 4.6% for the Canadian-born population.

The foreign-born population accounted for 45.7% of the CMA's total population of 5,072,100, up from 43.7% in 2001. (Toronto is the largest CMA in Canada, stretching from Ajax and

Pickering on the east to Milton on the west and
New Tecumseth and Georgina on the north.)

Four in every 10 new immigrants settled in the Toronto region

More foreign-born people settled in the Toronto
CMA between 2001 and 2006 than in any other
metropolitan area.

Of the total of 1,110,000 foreign-born people who
arrived in Canada during this five-year period, an
estimated 447,900, or 40.4%, chose Toronto. This
share was down slightly from the 43.1% of
newcomers who settled in Toronto in 2001. These
new immigrants made up 8.8% of Toronto's total
population in 2006.

The top two source countries for recent
immigrants to Toronto were Asian. In 2006, India
surpassed the People's Republic of China as the
number one source country of immigrants settling
in Toronto.

About 77,800 newcomers from India, 17.4% of all
newcomers, settled in the Toronto metropolitan
area. In addition, the census enumerated 63,900
newcomers, 14.3% of the total, from the People's
Republic of China. Combined, these two countries
accounted for nearly one-third of all newcomers
in the Toronto metropolitan area.

The new arrivals had a major impact on the
metropolitan area's workforce. An estimated
253,600, just over one-half (56.6%), were in the

prime working years, aged 25 to 54. They made up 10.8% of this age group in 2006.

Of the 789,400 school-aged children who were between 5 and 16 years old in the Toronto metropolitan area, recent immigrants made up 10.5%. Among these school-aged children, 54.9% reported speaking a non-official language most often at home.

More than two-thirds (68.5%) of newcomers in 2006 to the City of Toronto were born in Asian countries. The top five source countries of these recent immigrants were the People's Republic of China, India, the Philippines, Pakistan and Sri Lanka.

Chinese, including the different dialects, such as Mandarin and Cantonese, was reported by 17.3% of the newcomers as the language most often spoken at home. Another 4.8% of newcomers spoke Urdu most often at home.

Among the newcomers in the City of Toronto, about one-quarter (24%) spoke English most often at home. However, 1 in 10 reported that they did not have knowledge of either English or French.

Working-aged newcomers (between 25 and 54 years old) accounted for 58.7% of all recent immigrants who had resided in Toronto during the past five years.

In addition, 47,400 school-aged newcomers settled in the City of Toronto between 2001 and 2006. They accounted for 14.3% of all school-aged children in the city.

Markham: Second-highest proportion of foreign-born among Canadian municipalities

In 2006, 56.5% of the population in Markham was foreign-born. Only the City of Richmond in the Vancouver census metropolitan area (CMA) had a higher proportion of foreign-born in Canada. The foreign-born accounted for 57.4% of Richmond's population.

A total of 18,900 newcomers who came to Canada between 2001 and 2006 chose to live in Markham. They represented just under 1 in 10 (7.2%) residents of Markham's in 2006.

Recent immigrants in Markham are adding to the already diverse population. In 2006, the vast majority (84.3%) of newcomers were born in Asia and the Middle East. All top five source countries were in Asia: the People's Republic of China, India, Sri Lanka, Pakistan and the Philippines.

Fully 8% of school-aged children 5 to 16 years in Markham were recent immigrants to Canada. About one-quarter of them reported Chinese as a language spoken most often at home.

Mississauga: Majority were born outside of Canada

Mississauga has taken in an increasing share of recent immigrants over the past decade. In 2001, 14.5% of all newcomers in the Toronto metropolitan area lived in Mississauga. The share grew to 16.7% of new immigrants in 2006. In comparison, 13.1% of the total population in the Toronto metropolitan area lived in Mississauga in 2006.

As a result, the proportion of the foreign-born population in Mississauga increased from just less than half (46.8%) in 2001 to just over half (51.6%) in 2006.

Mississauga is home to foreign-born people who come from all corners of the world. In 2006, the top five countries of birth of recent immigrants there were India, Pakistan, the Philippines, the People's Republic of China and South Korea. This pattern of migration is reflected in the diversity of the communities in Mississauga.

Brampton: Increasing share of recent immigrants

In 2006, close to one-half (47.8%) of the population in Brampton, or 206,200 individuals, was born outside of Canada. This was up from 39.9% five years ago in 2001.

The increase in the proportion of the foreign-born is largely a result of the number of recent immigrants settling in Brampton. A total of 42,900 recent immigrants came to Canada between 2001 and 2006 chose to live in Brampton.

In 2006, 9.6% of all newcomers to the Toronto metropolitan area lived in Brampton. Just 5 years prior, in 2001, Brampton was home to 5% of all recent immigrants to the Toronto area.

Recent immigrants to Brampton came from all over the world, but most (77.4%) were born in Asia and the Middle East. In fact, two-thirds of all recent immigrants there came from just three countries: India, Pakistan and the Philippines.

Jamaica and Nigeria were also among the top source countries for newcomers to Brampton. The vast majority (95.7%) of Brampton's population reported knowledge of English or French. The small proportion that did not have knowledge of one of the official languages was mainly made up of recent immigrants who had arrived within five years.

About 3 in 10 said that they spoke Punjabi most often at home. The use of Punjabi reflects the high number of recent immigrants from India and Pakistan who settled in Brampton.

The census enumerated 6,186,950 foreign-born in Canada in 2006.